Short Horror Stories

Volume 3

P.J. Blakey-Novis

Disclaimer: "This is a work of fiction. Names, characters, places, and incidents are products of the author's imagination and are used fictitiously. Any resemblance to actual events, locales, or persons, living or dead, is entirely coincidental."

Short Horror Stories Volume 3 © P.J. Blakey-Novis 2024
© Red Cape Publishing 2024

All rights reserved.

Cover design by Red Cape Graphic Design
www.redcapepublishing.com/red-cape-graphic-design

Contents

Rosebud Cottage	*1*
Alone No More	*17*
Something Foul on Floor Thirteen	*32*
The Pioneer	*54*
The Tom Booker Sessions	*71*
Break-In at St. Benedict's	*89*
Doomsday	*116*
The Long Con	*132*
Rise of a Fucking Superstar	*153*
Carver's Hill	*167*
Blurred and Fractured Memories	*190*
We Want to Sing You a Song	*202*
Sister Mary	*218*
Cassie and the Demon	*237*
Purgatory	*252*

Rosebud Cottage

Margaret Wilson sat in the Chesterfield armchair nursing a crystal tumbler filled with expensive gin and a few cubes of ice, while the radio (or wireless, as she still called it) filled the room with the sound of Beethoven. The music, alongside the popping and crackling of logs on the fire, almost drowned out the gut-wrenching sounds coming from beyond the window. Almost. Margaret was thankful the heavy floor-to-ceiling curtains prevented her from seeing outside, as well as stopping the monster from being able to see in, but she had no doubt that they both were fully aware of one another's existence.

A ritual had been formed each time the sun went down - Margaret would bolt all doors and windows before closing the curtains around the country cottage. She would light a fire, more for comfort than for warmth, turn on the radio, and pour a stiff drink to keep her nerves at bay. Gin and tonic had not had the required effect for long, and Margaret now found herself taking the gin straight.

If Margaret had said that she wasn't afraid then she would have been lying, but she was also stubborn. At ninety-two years old, she had no intention of leaving her home, the cottage in which she had been born. The scratching at the window was almost

Short Horror Stories Volume 3

imperceptible to begin with but soon built to a crescendo, as had happened every evening for the past three weeks. A furious scraping sound soon filled the room and Margaret tried to focus her gin-addled mind on the music. Previously, the scratching at the windows would build up, before it seemed as though the creature had given up and skulked back into the woods. Tonight was different.

Margaret set her jaw, willing the sound to stop, the glass in her hands trembling from both fear and old age. A few moments passed which felt like hours before there was silence. A silence she had expected, signalling the creature's retreat. Content that she had been left alone, Margaret stood on unsteady feet and took a step towards the radio to turn it off, intent on heading to bed. She let out a scream as the sound of shattering glass filled the now-silent room. The curtains blew inward, flapping noisily, and Margaret turned to run. She reached the bottom of the staircase before chancing a look behind her, which she regretted immediately.

Two huge arms had reached in through the window, seemingly oblivious to the shards of glass still jutting from the wooden frame. Margaret stood frozen in fear as the beast pulled its looming form into her living room. It raised itself up on its hind legs, mouth salivating as it gazed upon its prey. "Fuck you," Margaret muttered, accepting the futility of her situation as the beast's teeth sank into her shoulder.

For the last ten years, Jonathan had been desperate to move again. He'd thought that exchanging city life for a small town would reduce his stress levels and provide a slower pace of life, and he had been right, up to a point. But it wasn't slow enough - or, rather, there were still too many people about. All he really wanted in life was a nice home, nothing huge, for himself and his wife to start a family in. Just the two of them, somewhere remote. It had been difficult to accept that this idyllic life was beyond their means, with housing deep in the English countryside being just as expensive as in the cities.

Jonathan and Marie saved as best they could but both, if they'd been completely honest, felt as though their dream life was just a fantasy. Marie was desperate for a child, but Jonathan kept telling her to wait until they had their home in the country, insisting it would be a far better environment in which to raise a family. Marie began to wonder if Jonathan even wanted children; what if they never managed to move? What if she got too old to have children? At thirty-five she still had time but not if it meant waiting another decade.

Then it came. Marie called it a miracle and even Jonathan had to agree that it was a most fortuitous turn of events. If they had seen the listing any later then someone else would have snapped it up but Marie was

Short Horror Stories Volume 3

making the call before Jonathan had even finished reading the details.

Rosebud Cottage, situated in the heart of the Sussex Downs, requires a live-in caretaker. The two-bedroomed property comes with a large garden and ample parking for three cars. The interior is dated but well kept, with all the necessities as well as an open fire. The owners of Rosebud Cottage are looking for someone to maintain the property, in exchange for free accommodation. Ideally this would suit a retired gentleman, but the owners are open to suggestions. Please note that this is an unpaid position, but you would have no rent due. The cottage is in a very remote location, so a car is essential.

Marie had wandered off while on the phone, but Jonathan could still make out the excitement in her voice. He sat patiently, waiting for her to fill him in on the details, certain that she would have made a decision for the both of them already.

"Well?" he said, watching as she struggled to contain her excitement.

"The owners want to meet us," Marie squealed. "They said that because I was the first to call, they would meet up with us."

"So, nothing is definite yet?" Jonathan asked, immediately feeling as though he was destroying Marie's hopes. Her face hardened a little and she took a breath.

"Not definite, no. But it sounds good and I think they liked me. I told them that the opportunity suited us perfectly, with you

4

working from home and me raising a baby."

"And they were okay with us having children at this place?" Jonathan asked.

"The woman, Kathy I think, she paused when I said we were planning a baby but then said it'd be fine. They will go over all the details when we meet up tomorrow, so write down any questions you have for them." Marie grabbed a notepad and pen, before ordering Jonathan to make a pot of tea.

The couple approached the cottage after a forty-minute drive, fifteen minutes of which was due to getting lost, and both looked around admiringly. It was quaint and, from the outside at least, appeared just as it had been described. Rose bushes were lined up along three sides of the cottage, a large lawned area spread out from the front of the building, and the gravelled area on which they had parked was indeed large enough for three cars, possibly even four. The owner, Kathy, greeted them at the front door and showed them inside. Jonathan and Marie could not have felt more different to one another as they stepped onto the dusty doormat. While she looked around and saw the potential of a new home and a new life, Jonathan just stared into the gloom, his senses tuning to the odour. *What is that smell?* he wondered, wrinkling his nose.

Kathy led them through to the living room and directed them to take a seat on the Chesterfield settee, while she positioned

Short Horror Stories Volume 3

herself in the armchair. Before they could ask, she brought up the boarded window.

"We're not sure what happened, to be honest. It was shattered from the outside. Could have been kids." *Out here?* Jonathan wondered, doubting that rogue teenagers were this far out in the countryside. Kathy was full of smiles, but Jonathan saw something hiding beyond that, a look in her eyes which could have been a mixture of fear and guilt, of a secret she was keeping from them.

"So, Marie tells me you're planning to try for a baby soon?" Kathy asked, her eyes meeting Jonathan's.

"That's right," he replied, not offering any more information.

"Okay," Kathy continued, "Let me tell you a bit about the place and what we're looking for. Rosebud Cottage has been in my family for a very long time and was my grandmother's home until she recently passed away." Jonathan noticed Kathy look to her left, glancing towards the bottom of the stairs, at what appeared to be a new rug. *Perhaps the old lady had taken a fall*, he wondered. "Anyway, this place is too remote for my liking, and would be a nightmare for commuting. No one in the family wants to see it sold off, so it'll probably be rented out at some point. For now, we're just after someone who can enjoy the location and take care of the place."

"Why not rent it out now, for the income?"

6

Jonathan asked. "I mean, it could do with a spruce up but it's certainly habitable." Kathy looked away again, and this time Jonathan had no doubt she was hiding something.

"No one wants to take on the responsibility at the moment. I have two brothers who work in London, my parents moved to Canada years ago, and I barely have any time to do things I enjoy as it is. The place isn't costing us anything so really you'd be doing us all a favour," she explained. "You work from home, I understand?"

"He runs an online store," Marie said. "It works well, and he can do it all from here, aside from trips to the post office once a week." She turned to Jonathan before adding, "Maybe you can get the food shopping on a Monday too, then we wouldn't have to travel much."

The couple spent an hour at the property, being guided from room to room. No one denied that it needed cleaning and that most of the furniture was outdated, but it had charm. Once they had seen everything the cottage had to offer inside, they took a quick tour of the grounds. The rear of the building was unremarkable but there was something about the lawn that bugged Jonathan.

"Did your grandma drive?" he asked, studying the grass ahead of them.

"No, she gave that up years ago. She was in her nineties; it wouldn't have been safe to have her on the roads," Kathy said with a chuckle.

Short Horror Stories Volume 3

"Those marks," Jonathan said, pointing a few metres ahead of him, "I just wondered what made them." He took a few steps closer, followed by Marie and Kathy. Stretching across the grass were a series of uneven grooves, leading from the tree line in the distance all the way to where they were standing. They could well have led all the way up to the cottage but were unnoticeable on the gravelled area.

"Dunno," Kathy replied. "Could be anything." Her jolly persona was starting to slip, and she soon made her excuses to leave. "Have a chat about it and let me know later today if you want to go ahead. I think you'll really like it here."

"No bloody Wi-Fi!" Jonathan exclaimed on the way home. "You do know that's essential for me to work, right?"

"I'm sure we can get that sorted out," Marie replied, still grinning with excitement at the opportunity.

"Did you think there was anything … weird about Kathy? Like she was hiding something?" Jonathan asked nervously, fearful that Marie would think he was making excuses not to move.

"Not weird," Marie began, before pausing. "She was a little off, but I put that down to recently losing her Grandmother. And being in the house she had died in."

"Did she tell you that her Grandma had actually died in the house? She could have

P.J. Blakey-Novis

been in a care home or hospital." Marie seemed to think this over.

"No, I don't think she did. I must have assumed it was at the house. Not that it makes any difference."

"Depends how she died," Jonathan replied. "Kathy kept glancing at the new rug at the bottom of the stairs; I reckon that's where it happened. You know," he continued, letting his mind wander, "Kathy never actually said *how* her Grandma died."

"Jesus Christ!" Marie exclaimed. "She was in her nineties, so I'd guess it was old age."

"Or she fell down the stairs and landed where that rug is."

"So what? If you don't want to move in then you should say so now, but I don't see any reason not to. And don't say it's because someone died there; I'm sure someone has died in our house at some point in the last hundred years that it's been there." Jonathan had no response to this so just grunted, accepting that he was not going to win this time around.

Marie had called Kathy that evening to confirm they would take on the cottage. Jonathan struggled to hide his feelings of unease but every issue he raised Marie brushed off as unimportant. The lack of Wi-Fi was the only point she agreed on and was her only request when she spoke with Kathy.

They were told that they could move in as soon as they liked but decided to hold off for

Short Horror Stories Volume 3

a fortnight to allow time to pack and change address with everyone who needed to know. This time also meant that Kathy could have the Internet up and running, and the living room window could be replaced before they arrived. Marie trusted Kathy to do these things but Jonathan wasn't convinced. Something about the whole situation felt off. Little did he know just how big of a mistake they were making.

Kathy was true to her word and had installed a super-fast broadband connection. The window had been repaired and it appeared as though a cleaning crew had worked their way throughout the house, successfully removing the musty smell and freshening everything up. When they had arrived on that first day, a removals van following closely behind them, Jonathan realised that he now had nothing to complain about. Putting his worries aside, (worries that seemed to have no root in reality), he embraced the change of pace when he saw how truly happy Marie was. His mood was raised further by his wife's determination to become pregnant and her demands for him to impregnate her all around the cottage.

A month went by with the couple barely leaving the home. Aside from any necessary trips to the Post Office and supermarket on a Monday, the rest of their time was spent either working at the table out on the lawn or making love. On some of the warmer days they even tried for a baby in the garden, enjoying the privacy of being so far from any other people. It was on one of these warm evenings, as Marie and Jonathan fooled around on a picnic blanket on the grass, that they first encountered *it*.

"Did you hear something?" Marie asked over the sound of Jonathan's heavy breathing. He was too far into the moment to register what she had asked and continued with the task at hand. *Crack*. "There it is again," Marie said, this time attempting to wriggle out from beneath her husband.

"What?" Jonathan asked, looking around. "There's no-one here."

"I heard something, like someone had stood on a twig and snapped it." Marie's eyes darted across the tree line at the end of the lawn. "I think someone is watching us."

"Don't be silly," Jonathan replied. He briefly though back to Kathy's suggestion that kids had broken the living room window but decided not to mention it. "Would you rather we take this inside?"

"Yes please," Marie answered. "I don't like the idea of some pervert watching us." Jonathan shrugged, as though he didn't really care either way. Pulling on enough clothing to conceal themselves, the couple lifted the blanket from the ground and turned to head indoors. *Crack*.

"I heard it that time," Jonathan said, scanning the trees for any signs of an

Short Horror Stories Volume 3

intruder. His faced showed no fear but there was a definite hint of anger. "You go inside. I'll go take a look. If it's a group of kids I'll send them packing." Jonathan flicked on the flashlight app on his mobile phone, as Marie wrapped the blanket around herself and waited at the front door, watching the light bounce across the grass in time with Jonathan's steps.

Jonathan reached the trees and called out with a *hello*. No answer. Marie watched as he shone the light into the trees, pacing along the edge of the lawn. She could make out his silhouette as he turned back towards the house. She watched Jonathan shrug once more, hands out in front of him as though he were telling her he'd found nothing. She watched as the area of grass behind him became darker and something emerged from the trees. Jonathan must have heard it, or sensed it at least, because he turned at the same time that Marie screamed.

No more than six feet from him, the beast stood on two hind legs. It's black fur barely visible in the dark of night, Jonathan's eyes were drawn to the parts which he could see clearly - the eyes and the mouth. At six feet tall, Jonathan was not a short man, but he had to look up to meet the glare of this creature. Mouth open, spilling drool from around deadly-looking fangs, the creature took a swipe at Jonathan. He leapt back a step, narrowly missing being struck by the beast's clawed hands. Turning again towards

P.J. Blakey-Novis

the cottage, he ran.

Marie stood screaming at the entrance to the house, petrified beyond words. She watched as this hideous thing had emerged from the within the trees and loomed over her husband, as it swiped at him with its claws. Marie registered that Jonathan was running towards her, that they needed to get into the house, but she could not move. The seconds felt like minutes as he approached her, and she watched helplessly as the beast gained on him. She watched him fall forwards as though he'd been shoved from behind and fully expected the creature to kill him right there and then. So, when the thing leapt over Jonathan and kept its course towards Marie, she was caught off-guard.

Acting on impulse, Marie darted inside and slammed the front door, clicking the lock into place. At the speed it had been moving, she had expected the creature to slam into the door but there was nothing more than a spray of gravel as it came to a stop outside. An acceptance of their situation hit Marie and she began to act on autopilot, moving around the house to turn off lights whilst simultaneously trying to find something to use as a weapon.

The kitchen knife she held in her shaking hands would do her little good against a beast of that size, and she knew this, but it had to be better than nothing. Cautiously, she peered through the living room window, the one which had been recently replaced.

Short Horror Stories Volume 3

Whatever that thing was, it was pacing about on the lawn, more interested in the cottage than in Jonathan. Marie watched her husband try to stand a few times but could see that he was injured. All he could manage was a pitiful attempt at crawling and he wasn't even going the right way. *He should be coming to me!* she thought, wondering if he was disorientated. Then it hit her. *He's heading for the car! He's going to leave.*

Marie watched Jonathan crawl across the lawn, wondering whether he would really desert her. *He must expect me to join him,* she thought, watching the creature continue to pace and trying to decide if she'd make it to the car before that thing could get to her. Reluctantly, she opened the front door and looked across at Jonathan's car. He was making steady progress and it seemed as if the monster had forgotten he was even there. Jonathan stopped to roll onto his back and fumbled in his pockets, pulling out his keys. Marie could see exactly what was about to happen but could do nothing to stop it. *You're too far away still,* she wanted to yell, but knew that screaming out would be suicide.

Jonathan turned his head towards the doorway in which his wife stood and nodded, holding the keys up. She would never be able to drag him the rest of the way to the car, certainly not before that creature was upon them. Marie shook her head, feeling the tears begin to drop. Jonathan nodded again and

P.J. Blakey-Novis

pressed the button.

There was a flash of orange as the car's indicator lights signalled that it had been unlocked. The creature stopped pacing and turned its head to the source of the lights. Marie bolted, running as fast as she could, focussing only on the keys in Jonathan's outstretched hand. She heard panting coming from behind her, getting closer, close enough to feel the warmth of breath on the back of her neck. She lunged, scooping up the keys just as Jonathan let out a scream.

Whether or not the beast was running for her or Jonathan, Marie could not tell, but his scream had undoubtedly been to get its attention. He had done that for her. Clambering into the car she caught a glimpse in the rear-view mirror and her stomach turned. The creature's head was almost fully immersed into Jonathan's torso, devouring every organ it could find. Marie started the car and pushed the lever into Drive. She paused, her husband's death hitting her with force. A new idea formed in Marie's mind and she grabbed the lever once more, putting the car into reverse and slamming her foot to the floor. Gravel sprayed as the car careened backwards onto the lawn. There was a sickening thud as the wheels bumped over the remains of Jonathan, but she had not hit the beast.

Checking each of the mirrors, she could not see the creature. *Has it disappeared into the woods again?* she wondered. Marie flicked

15

Short Horror Stories Volume 3

on the headlights, illuminating the entire lawn. As though it had been a shadow, able to hide in the absence of light, the monster stood before her. It leapt at the same instant Marie accelerated but the high roof of the 4x4 caught its legs, sending it sprawling to the ground. Marie spun the car around as quickly as she could, driving into the beast before it could get back on its feet, and sending it flying across the grass and onto the gravel near the front door to the cottage. Marie struck again, this time misjudging her speed. The car went over the creature with a wet, cracking sound but Marie could not stop before the car plunged through the wall and into the living room. Ancient bricks crumbled around the vehicle as the airbags exploded into Marie's face. Dazed, she shoved at the door to free herself from the wreckage.

Stepping onto the gravel she took in the mess which lay before her. Matted fur, crushed bones, and bloody entrails littered the exterior of the cottage and Marie's first thought made her laugh. "What is Kathy going to say about this?" she muttered, before everything clicked into place. *Kathy's secret, her Grandma's suspicious death, the broken window, the marks on the grass.*

Certain that Jonathan's 4x4 was now a write-off, Marie headed to the kitchen to retrieve the keys to her own car and checked the paperwork for Kathy's address. *She has some questions to answer,* Marie thought, filled with rage. The beast would not be the

only one to bleed at the hands of Marie that
night.

Alone No More

I was five when I met him. He was older. It's impossible to know by how much, time works differently for his kind. He looked only a little bigger than me, certainly not a grown up. He still looks that way. It's odd to think back now, twenty years later. Being so innocent at that age, I told my parents all about my new 'friend'. They couldn't see him, dismissing him as a child's imaginary playmate. I recall the confusion I felt, knowing he was real, but I was also at the age when I believed my parents to be entirely correct, all of the time. I didn't have the clarity of mind to wonder if I was mentally ill. Now, I spend some days certain that I must be insane, and others when I know I'm right. In a world filled with betrayal and disappointment, he has been with me through it all. The thought he was responsible for most of my heartache never made it to the forefront until *that* night when everything changed. But, I suppose, it had been lingering somewhere in my mind, a darkness clawing at me, for some time.

I was five, as I'd mentioned. I found him in the attic of our new house when I was exploring. I hadn't wanted to move but the old house made Mum sad. I'd had a brother, but he died when he was really small. My only memories of him are from a couple of

P.J. Blakey-Novis

photos. So my parents packed us up and moved us a few towns over. I remember feeling sad too when Ollie died but kids are resilient. It sounds awful but I got over it pretty quickly. I guess they thought I'd made up my new friend as some kind of coping mechanism, but it was nothing that predictable. I mean, I was five. I'd never heard the word Djinn before.

I was never afraid of him, perhaps because he wasn't much older than I was at the time, but it did strike me as odd that he'd be there. Dad had been putting some of our things into the attic but the previous owners had left a load of junk, so he was in a mood. I remember hearing him moaning at Mum about all the extra hassle. As a child, the attic was exciting (we hadn't had one at the old house), and with it full of potential treasure I was up the ladder before anyone could notice. The way my dad was going on, I'd expected it to be filled to the roof. What I actually found was a neat pile of maybe six or seven large cardboard boxes. There was no sudden discovery of my friend – he didn't pop out of a box, he didn't suddenly shout from a dark corner. He was simply there, his back resting against the boxes, a fidget spinner balancing on one blue finger.

"Hi," I said, eyes fixed on the toy. "I'm Alice." He looked up at me and smiled, I remember it so clearly. It was a friendly smile, I could tell that much, and even at my young age I could sense the sadness in it.

19

Short Horror Stories Volume 3

"Hi," he replied, catching the spinner as it fell from his finger.

"What's your name?" I asked but he just looked at the floor and frowned. He told me he didn't have a name, or, if he did, he couldn't remember it. I named him Ollie, after my brother. Another reason my parents thought I was making it all up. We played for a while, taking turns with the fidget spinner, pulling assorted bric-a-brac from the boxes as I searched for anything worth keeping. Eventually, I asked him the most important question my five-year-old mind could come up with.

"Why are you blue?"

"Why are you pink?" he replied with a shrug. *Touché,* I would have thought, had I known the word. After a pause, he began to explain that he was a Djinn. I must have looked confused as I thought I'd heard my mum say that was a drink for grown-ups. "Genie?" he asked, testing to see if I knew *that* word. I grinned.

"Aren't you supposed to live in a lamp?" I asked. He just laughed. "Do you grant wishes?"

"It's not like that," he told me. And it really wasn't. He had, no, *has*, powers. Whether he uses them to help some poor human get what they want is entirely up to him. I recall a feeling of disappointment – no lamp to rub, no three wishes. But I did have a new friend.

As I've said, my parents didn't exactly believe me, but they let me get on with it. I'd

P.J. Blakey-Novis

play in the attic, with their permission, taking games and toys up there. Sometimes they would set me up to sleep in there too. Most of my time, outside of school hours, was spent in that dusty room. If my parents were worried about me, they kept it to themselves, wallowing in their own misery. I didn't ask for anything from Ollie until I was eleven.

Secondary school had crept up on me. I had a few friends in my class but I never socialised outside of school, preferring to play board games in the attic. I'd been at the new school a week when I ran into Becky. She hadn't been at my primary school, (everyone there had been quite nice), so I wasn't expecting to come across anyone like her. She shoved me over on the playground, for no reason that I could think of. I told a teacher, as that's how I'd been taught to respond to bullies. This had made it worse; Becky singled me out and made my school life unbearable for weeks – name-calling, throwing food at me, pushing me about. My parents said they'd speak to the school, but nothing changed. I told Ollie, he was my only real friend, and he listened. He cared.

Aside from upset and afraid, Becky had made me feel anger, possibly for the first time ever. I didn't realise I'd said it until the words had left my mouth. "I wish Becky was dead." Ollie was staring at me, a slight rise in the corners of his mouth. A smile?

"Okay," he said. I didn't think any more of it.

Short Horror Stories Volume 3

Becky wasn't at school the next day, or ever again. Death by misadventure was the official verdict. Messing about on the railway lines seemed like the sort of thing Becky would do so I'd just put it down to an unfortunate accident. If I'd known any different at the time, I wonder if I'd really have cared.

I was fourteen when I started noticing boys. I mean, properly noticing. Ollie was my closest friend and we spent every moment together that we could, but he never would leave that damn attic. He felt like the brother I'd lost; there was certainly no romantic interest from my side. Things with my parents were weird, but it's hard to describe. It's as though they had given up on me, or that's how it felt. I rarely mentioned Ollie to them but after almost ten years of me playing with *someone* in the attic, they seemed to accept it as a quirk. I suppose I feel that they should have taken me to a therapist if they'd really cared. Not that it would have helped; Ollie was, and still is, as real as I am.

So, boys. There was one in my class, Matt, that I had a bit of a crush on. I never told him, or anyone at all, but Ollie knew. Perhaps I'd mentioned Matt more times in conversation than I'd realised and Ollie sensed something. One rainy Saturday, playing chess with Ollie, he asked me if I'd ever leave. I didn't know what to say, I hadn't thought that far ahead.

"It'll be a few years before I can move out,"

I said, too young to want to think about adulthood.

"But then you'll leave..." Ollie replied, and I could see the sadness there. "Just like Marcie did."

"Who's Marcie?" I asked. Ollie had never mentioned anyone else in all the years we had been playing together.

"She lived here before you came," he explained. "We played together too but her parents weren't like yours. They frightened her. She'd stay up here with me for weeks to avoid them."

"And then they moved? You couldn't go with them?" I asked.

Ollie shook his head. "Marcie wished she didn't have to live with them anymore. She has a new family now."

"Oh," was all I could manage, not really following but content it seemed like a happy ending, for Marcie at least. "So, you can't leave?" I asked. It struck me hard that I'd never thought about this before, happily heading down for dinner, or off to bed, leaving Ollie here, in the dark and alone.

"My wishes don't count. Marcie never wished for me to be able to leave this room, so I couldn't. It's that simple."

"So, if I wished you were able to come outside with me, then you could?" I asked, excitement growing. "You could meet my parents, show them that I'm not imagining you!"

"No!" Ollie said, fear gripping his face. "I

Short Horror Stories Volume 3

can only be seen when I choose to be, and humans are trouble for my kind."

I frowned. "I'm a human," I pointed out with a small smile.

"You're a child. Humans, adult ones, took my parents, trapped them in jars, used them for their powers. My father bound me to this place to keep me safe and I have been. I shouldn't leave, even if I want to."

"Come out with me," I pleaded. "I wish you'd come outside with me." Ollie gave a nod of his head but looked petrified. "Oh shit, I *wished* it. Now you have to come!" Excitedly, I climbed out of the attic and looked up through the hatch. Ollie was there, blue legs dangling through the opening, his face creased with worry. For a moment I felt guilty, having forced him to take this step, but reasoned that it must be in his best interest.

Cautiously, I led him along the hallway and down the stairs. "Can anyone else see you?" I whispered. He shook his head and I let out a sigh of relief. Mum was in the kitchen which had a clear view of the front door. I slipped my shoes on, watching to see if she'd notice me. She did.

"Where are you off to?" she asked.

"Just wanted to get out for a bit, thought I'd grab a magazine."

"It's raining!" Mum pointed out. I shrugged and wrapped a coat around me.

"Won't be long," I called, stepping out into the street.

P.J. Blakey-Novis

I looked at Ollie and he grabbed my hand. For such a powerful being, he certainly seemed uncomfortable out of the attic. "If no one can see you then you've got nothing to worry about. We won't be long, anyway." This earned me a glare from a man walking past us and I reminded myself that it looked as though I was alone; perhaps I shouldn't talk so loudly.

We reached the shop and ducked in out of the rain. I remember it clearly for two reasons – it was the first time Ollie had been outside, and it was when the possibilities really hit me. I'd gone in with the intention of buying a magazine and a large bar of chocolate, which I did. There was nothing else in the corner store that I was interested in, so we left. Something in the window of the repair shop opposite caught my eye. I'd been asking for a new laptop for a while, but it hadn't been forthcoming. It wasn't out of any sense of greed, but the bulky (not to mention extremely slow) one I had for school was getting noticed. It wasn't 'cool' enough and, as much as I hate to admit it, this did bother me. I'd had five pounds in the entire world, before the magazine and chocolate bar. This was now a little over a pound. *Only £149 short...*I thought.

"I wish I had enough money for a new laptop," I said, deliberately looking away from Ollie. I caught him nod out of the corner of my eye and checked my pockets, half-expecting to find a wad of notes in there.

Short Horror Stories Volume 3

Nothing. Not wanting to press the issue with Ollie, fearing he would think I was using him, I turned to leave. A knock on the shop window made me turn and I saw the owner reaching around the display. The £150 price ticket had been crossed out. *Reduced, now £1.* I looked at Ollie but he didn't make eye contact. I think I'd offended him somehow but I still rushed into the shop and bought the device.

We walked home in silence as I tried to come up with a believable reason for me to have the laptop. I could explain it was reduced to a pound, not untrue, but it still sounds rather suspicious. Coming up short, I did the obvious thing. I wished my parents wouldn't notice the new laptop.

Things changed from then on, but I'm not sure they were for the better.

I wished for popularity and people at school started being nicer to me. Matt asked me out on a date but I said no... nerves, perhaps. I wished for more money for myself and my parents. Dad got a pay rise and my allowance went up. These changes weren't huge and it's possible they were unrelated to my wishes, in the same way fortune tellers will give vague enough information to make it almost believable. Aside from the laptop, my wishes had been small and quite reasonable. Ollie showed no sign of disapproval or otherwise, so I carried on. But greed is a human thing.

By sixteen, I'd become lazy at school.

P.J. Blakey-Novis

Thinking back, I regret not wishing that I knew the answers to the exam questions rather than simply wishing for good grades. At least I would have had the knowledge, but trigonometry hasn't been required so far in my adult life. To be honest, the grades didn't matter anyway. I can have whatever I like.

I wouldn't say Ollie is in love with me, but dependent is certainly true. I moved out at eighteen, after a 'miraculous' lotto win. I bought a sensible, small house for Ollie and myself. Things were going well. I'd travel, with Ollie, of course, and those first couple of years were a real adventure. I'd met Javier at a ski resort when I was twenty. He was older, handsome, clearly wealthy. I lost my virginity to him, (late, I know, but Ollie was always watching), ignoring his wedding ring. Ollie's presence was something I knew I'd have to block out at some point and that night I wished for him to stay away from me for a few hours. It worked – he was gone for precisely three hours. When he returned, he was a wreck.

I felt awful... ashamed, even. Here was my friend, still the size of a seven-year-old, crying terribly. I decided that we needed to talk. I tried to explain how much I cared for Ollie, but that sometimes, (such as with Javier), I needed a little privacy. Ollie didn't understand. He genuinely couldn't grasp any middle ground between being together all the time, or never seeing one another again. I put this down to the loss of his parents but knew

Short Horror Stories Volume 3

something would have to give. His tone had lost its usually friendliness when he gave me an ultimatum.

"If you want me to go, I will. If you've got everything you want from me. But the wishes go with me. Everything you've had from me gets wiped away." I was certain he was bluffing but even so, I didn't want to lose him.

"It's not like that," I said, trying to plan my words before letting them escape. "Everything I've asked for has been to benefit *us*. It's meant that we can be together freely in that house, that we can travel."

"What happens if you meet a good man and want to settle down?" Ollie asked. The question had been kicking around in my head for a while and I had no answer for him. "I'll get replaced. I don't want that to happen." The glint in his eyes told me that he wouldn't go willingly and, for the first time in fifteen years, I was afraid of Ollie.

"I don't think there *are* any good men, so don't worry about it at the moment," I said, trying to lighten the mood.

"Am I not a good man?" Ollie asked.

"Of course you are," I replied, before understanding where this was leading.

"You could wish for me to be a man. You could wish me to be whatever kind of man you wanted. Then I could do those things that Javier did to you."

I felt my cheeks redden. "I can't do that," I said, not believing my own words. I knew that

28

P.J. Blakey-Novis

I *could* do it, but did I really want to?

"Why not? I'd happily give up my powers to be with you, to be a human couple with you. It would be perfect."

"It isn't right," I said, shaking my head. "If your powers were gone, there would be no going back."

"Going back to what? I can't wish for anything for myself. All I have is you." Ollie's desperation was evident and I felt, for the first time, the weight of responsibility for him. I had choices to make but doubted my ability to be selfless.

"I'll be honest with you," I began slowly. "I only see a few options for the future. We should discuss them – it shouldn't all be on me to tell you what happens." Ollie was watching me; I could swear he was nervous. "We can stay as we are, having adventures, living like this. But it feels unfair to both of us. I don't want you to feel pushed aside if I meet someone important to me." No reaction from Ollie but he stared at me intently. "We can go with your idea, you become human, we see where that takes us. But I make no promises. It doesn't mean we'll be together forever."

"I'd never leave you," Ollie said.

"I know," I replied, waiting for him to understand. I sighed.

"Any other suggestions?" Ollie asked. I shook my head. The scenario in which we part ways wasn't going to work for either of us.

Short Horror Stories Volume 3

"Aside from you becoming human, what else would you wish for?" I asked. "If you could have one wish come true."

"I can't make wishes."

"I know, I was just wondering. Hypothetically," I said, forcing a smile. These decisions were too big and I just wanted to carry on as we had been, at least for a while longer. Ollie remained silent but appeared to be thinking. "If I wished for you to be able to make one wish that would come true, aside from the one where you become human, would it work?"

Ollie's eyes fixed on me, a grin forming on his blue face. "I have no idea," he said with a smile. "But we can give it a go."

"I wish Ollie could make one wish for himself, with the exception of becoming human," I said. I saw him nod. I watched a sly smile cross his face, his eyes narrowing. He nodded again.

"What did you wish for?" I asked, butterflies forming in my stomach.

"Happiness," he replied, but there was something more that he wasn't saying. I could detect a smirk trying to form on his blue face.

"What have you done?" I said, my voice beginning to tremble. Ollie pointed to a mirror. I glance at my reflection and screamed.

I soon discovered that Ollie had never been entirely honest with me about the way things

P.J. Blakey-Novis

worked. It was true that he could not make wishes which came true, without my permission. It was true that I could have as many wishes granted as I wanted. Perhaps it wasn't dishonesty, but more like missing out an important point. Ollie was not obligated to grant a wish. It was down to his discretion and now he was using his power over me.

I was unrecognisable in my reflection. My clear skin and youthful looks had been replaced by something diseased and rotten – I looked as though I were in the late stages of leprosy. Chunks of skin around my neck and cheeks were flaking away in red, pus-filled strands. My bloodshot eyes only showed fear and, as I opened my mouth in terror, my teeth appeared black and about to drop out. I looked at my hands – they appeared as they had been before. Holding them up to the mirror, they, too, looked desiccated and destroyed. I put a hand to my face, expected to feel the wet roughness of weeping scabs but all felt as it should. *An illusion,* I realised.

"What have you done?" I shouted. Ollie stared, his eyes hard, no regret showing.

"You're beautiful," he said. I shuddered.

"Why am I seeing...*that?*" I pointed to the mirror. "Is it a threat? Is that what I'll become if I don't make you human? You really think I'll allow you more wishes?" I was almost screaming at Ollie now, his betrayal cutting me deep.

"*I* still see you as you really are," Ollie stated. The emphasis on *I* took me a moment

Short Horror Stories Volume 3

to understand.

"But I'm forced to see that monster when I look in a mirror? Why?"

"No," Ollie said, shaking his head. "Look again."

Hesitantly, I looked at the mirror and saw myself, my real self. I let out a sigh of relief, allowing myself to believe it had been a cruel trick and nothing more. "What was the point in that? You said you wished for happiness – how does scaring me like that make you happy?"

"*I* still see you as you really are," Ollie repeated. "I suppose I should say *we*, really." I stared blankly at the blue boy, sensing an evil growing within him. Perhaps it had always been there. "Only *we* see you that way. Everyone else sees *that* version of you."

"I wish that everyone could see me as I really look," I blurted out quickly. There was no nod of Ollie's head. "I wish you had never made that wish!" Still no nod. "I wish I'd never fucking met you!" I screamed.

Ollie smiled. "Don't say things you don't mean. This is for the best."

"How do I know you're telling the truth?" I asked. "For all I know that was just a trick."

"Fancy a walk?" Ollie asked, gesturing towards the door with a grin. We'd taken two steps onto the street when I knew he wasn't lying. My appearance led to horrified gasps, diverted eyes, pity-filled looks.

"Please," I began, not really knowing what I could say. "Don't leave me like this."

P.J. Blakey-Novis

"I'll never leave you," Ollie replied with a shrug. "You're the reason for my happiness. And please don't worry about the way people see you. I just wanted to make sure nobody else would love you."

Tears ran down my cheeks as the reality set in. There was no going back from this; Ollie had won. I could not escape him and, even if I did, I'd be alone. Would that be worse?

Short Horror Stories Volume 3

Something Foul on Floor Thirteen

When Nancy moved into Castle Heights a little over a year ago, she thought it was a shithole. But she was well aware that on her nurse's salary and having found herself suddenly single, a shithole was all she could afford. If someone were to ask her now what she thought of the place, with its peeling wallpaper, worn and suspiciously stained carpets, and bizarre odour that nobody could quite identify, she'd still call it a dump - but it was *her* dump.

Castle Heights, as grandiose as the name may have sounded, was far from being a palace. But as they say, an Englishman's (or English*woman*'s) home is their castle. What Nancy found was a community of sorts, not a heap of concrete stuffed with junkies and layabouts as she had expected. Her parents had never been to visit and had gone so far as to advise Nancy not to take the place. However, as they weren't offering to contribute to anywhere more suitable, they had little influence over the decision. Nancy told them about the flat, mentioning that it was number 81, but omitting the fact it was on floor thirteen. Her superstitious mother would likely have a heart attack if she knew that.

Within a matter of weeks, Nancy had met the occupants of her floor. Well, most of

P.J. Blakey-Novis

them. Apartment 81 was at one end of the corridor, with 86 at the other end. She'd had conversations with the elderly couple at 82, shared wine with Jane, the single mother at 83, ogled the two men from number 84 who were undoubtedly uninterested in women, and exchanged pleasantries with Herbert, the overweight but kindly middle-aged man at number 85. Nancy had never seen anyone go in or out of the flat at the end of the corridor. None of her neighbours had mentioned the inhabitants so she had presumed it to be vacant. Until tonight.

As a nurse, Nancy worked shifts, of course. She would come and go at all hours, allowing her to pick up on the routines of her neighbours. Maureen and Edgar at 82 hardly ever left the building. They rarely were awake past 8pm either, as Nancy had discovered one evening when she had knocked on their door, looking to borrow some milk, just before 9. Edgar had eventually made it out of bed and to the door as Nancy was re-entering her own apartment. Nancy apologised, of course, but Edgar was in good spirits. "We get to bed early these days," he'd explained. "Best not to be about too late, especially on this floor." What Nancy had taken as a joke at the time should have been heeded as a warning.

Jane from 83 was back and forth, sometimes carting her screaming toddler along to the lift and down to the play park

Short Horror Stories Volume 3

nearby. She had been quite forthcoming about her situation when they'd shared drinks, how she'd got herself knocked up by her married boss who then suggested she find new employment. Nancy would bump into the men at 84 if she was on an early shift, often riding the lift with them to the ground floor. She'd never got around to asking what they did, but they were always sharply dressed by 7am and seemed to be heading to work. Herbert, on the other hand, did not work. His large frame required him to walk with a cane and Nancy would hear him wheezing along the corridor if he had the urge to leave the building, usually for cigarettes and a newspaper.

That just left apartment 86...the source of something rather foul.

Nancy had worked what she called a middle shift. These were by far her favourite as they were close to what could be called 'normal' working hours, albeit a long day still. She'd left a little after ten, taken the short bus ride to the hospital, and began her duties by 11am. Things were always busy and she ate little, rushing between patients. She told herself that busy was good, it made the time go faster, and before she knew it, 9pm had arrived. A 9pm finish does not always mean that, however, and Nancy found herself attending to one last patient before she could make her getaway, just missing the bus she would normally catch.

P.J. Blakey-Novis

She waited in the cold for the next twenty minutes, before slumping into a seat on the bus, now thinking about food. Aware there was little available in her apartment, Nancy decided to stop at the corner store for snacks and well-needed alcohol. Tomorrow was a day off, a rare treat in itself, and she planned to drink a bottle or two of wine and sleep for as long as possible.

Nancy made it off the bus, in and out of the shop, and almost to the entrance of Castle Heights before things took a turn.

"Cold night," said a man's voice, a few feet from the main door. Nancy glanced up, seeing a figure in a black suit smoking a cigarillo, his dark hat concealing most of his face.

"Sure is," she muttered, reaching out for the door.

"I need to come in...would you mind?" the man said, stepping towards Nancy.

"You live here?" she asked, certain she had never seen him before.

"No. Just visiting..." he explained.

"You'll need to buzz whoever you're visiting to let you in then." Nancy opened the door, her stomach turning, fearful the man may try to follow.

"Tried that - no reply."

"What flat number? I'll let the concierge know and he can check they're home."

"Very kind of you," he said, tipping his hat a little. "Apartment 86, Floor 13."

Nancy made it through the door, closing it

Short Horror Stories Volume 3

before the man followed, but she could have sworn he said, 'thank you, Nancy'.

The ground floor was gloomy, the build-up of dust, dead flies, and grime on the lamp shades keeping the entire building in a state of dimly lit neglect. On a chair sat Trevor, the concierge, somehow managing to read a newspaper in the poor light.

"Trevor," Nancy called.

"Nancy!" he replied in his thick Scottish brogue. "How are you this evening?"

"I'm fine, thanks. There's a guy outside, said he's visiting someone in 86 but they aren't answering. I told him I'd let you know." Nancy detected a flash of something in Trevor's eyes, fear perhaps, but it vanished in an instant.

"Okay, dear. I'll go and have a chat with him." Trevor folded his paper slowly, seeming to be in no hurry to get out of his chair. Nancy headed towards one of the two lifts before pausing.

"I thought 86 was empty?" she asked. "I've never heard a sound from there."

"Well, nothing wrong with quiet neighbours, is there?" Trevor replied with a shrug. Nancy stepped into the lift and watched Trevor open the main entrance before she hit the button for floor thirteen.

As the lift doors parted, Nancy almost dropped her bag of wine and snacks. She'd taken the lift at her end of the building, so it opened outside of her apartment's door but, even in the gloom, there was no mistaking

38

P.J. Blakey-Novis

what she saw. A crack of light illuminated the carpet at the end of the corridor, spilling from the door to number 86. Not only did it light up the floor, but it shined off the black shoes, the black suit, and that damned black hat of the man standing there. Nancy's mind reeled, wondering how he had gotten there before her, and with genuine surprise that flat 86 was indeed inhabited.

The conversation the man was having was too faint to be heard from where Nancy stood, but as she took a step out of the lift, her wine bottles clinked together loudly. She may as well have shouted, the sound shattering the quiet and drawing the man's attention to her. Unable to take her eyes away from him, Nancy took the few steps to her front door and fumbled for her keys. If he had been in conversation, that had been cut short. Now, he just stared at Nancy. She matched his glare but felt her heart racing, as though she were in danger, as though the entire population of Castle Heights was now at risk. Nancy looked away from the stranger to find the keyhole. As she turned her key in the lock, she risked a final glance back and paused. She hadn't heard the door close, but the man was gone, the door to 86 was shut tight, and all was silent. Once inside, Nancy slid across the chain on her door and began running a hot shower, an anxious feeling gnawing at her.

Once she'd showered and slipped on a

Short Horror Stories Volume 3

clean nightdress, Nancy made herself comfortable on the sofa with an open bottle of wine and an assortment of crisps and chocolate. Deciding she was too tired to read, she flicked on the television, scrolling through for some late-night horror movie to watch. Time had little meaning for Nancy, she would work, chill out for a couple of hours, and then sleep - whether that was midday, or the early hours of the morning, it made no difference. It was a little past 11pm by the time Nancy found something to watch, a low-budget TV movie with some kind of sea monsters, and she'd made a dent in the first bottle of wine half an hour later.

The first scream came at 11.34pm. Nancy knew the exact time as she glanced at the clock instinctively. For a moment, she assumed it had come from the movie and wondered if she should turn down the volume for the sake of her neighbours. A minute later, a second scream rang out. This time the television was on a commercial break.

What the fuck? Nancy wondered, muting the television. Frozen in place, she listened intently for any other sounds, for someone else to go into the corridor to investigate. Five minutes passed in silence, Nancy barely dared to breathe, when another sound came. It was more than a scream, it was the sound of true terror, as though every damned soul in Hell itself was calling to her for help. There was a fraction of a second of silence before

P.J. Blakey-Novis

everything went dark and Nancy let out a scream of her own.

The silence was oppressive. There had been power outages at Castle Heights in the past, more so than with most buildings due to its poor maintenance, but usually it would only last for minutes. Often, people would congregate in the hallways and check on one another. Nancy sat in silent darkness, listening for any sign of movement but hearing nothing. She reached for her phone, flicking on the flashlight app. If it hadn't been for the screaming, Nancy would have just resigned herself to bed but there was no denying something was going on. And she was well aware she'd be unable to sleep if she didn't at least check on her neighbours.

Certain that Maureen and Edgar would be asleep and oblivious to the situation, Nancy slowly opened her front door. She flicked it onto the catch, pocketed her keys just in case, and took a few cautious steps along the corridor. Still no sounds. She wondered if she should really be knocking on anyone's doors at this hour - for all she knew, they were all sound asleep. Nancy hovered outside Jane's flat, deciding to text instead.

Hey, power went out. U ok? Was gonna knock but didn't want 2 wake Charlie.

A moment passed without reply and Nancy took another step along the corridor. Her phone was on silent but still vibrated so, when a call from Jane came through, Nancy let out another scream of her own.

Short Horror Stories Volume 3

"Jesus!" she muttered, swiping the screen to answer. "Jane...I'm outside your..." Nancy dropped the phone as the haunting screams of tortured souls echoed through the receiver. "Oh shit!"

Fearing Jane may be in trouble, Nancy began pounding on the door. Nothing about the situation was all right, nothing felt safe or even made any sense, and Nancy couldn't stop the tears from falling. After what felt like an eternity, Jane's door opened a little, the security chain holding it back.

"Nancy? What's wrong? Oh my God, has something happened to you?"

"I...You...called me..." Nancy stuttered, confusion swelling. "The power went out. Did you hear all the screaming?"

"I didn't hear anything, I was asleep. Probably just teenagers messing about outside."

"It wasn't outside. I texted you to see if you were okay, and then you called me, but it wasn't you."

"You're not making any sense. I haven't touched my phone - like I said, I was asleep." Jane removed the chain from the door and opened it wider. "Look, I'm up now, want a coffee?"

"No power for coffee," Nancy said, looking nervously up and down the hallway before following Jane in anyway. Jane flicked a few switches and verified that the power was out, before using Nancy's phone to light the way to her bedroom and retrieving her own

P.J. Blakey-Novis

device.

"It's not even switched on," Jane stated, her concern for her neighbour evident. Nancy explained the events thus far; the strange man waiting outside, how he had been on their floor visiting 86, the power cut, the screams, the phone call. "That's not all that weird," Jane replied, her shrug just about visible in the darkness.

"Seems pretty odd to me," Nancy said.

"What? Someone lives at 86, they just happen to be quiet. They had a visitor. That lift moves quicker than the one you took. There was a power cut. All pretty explainable..."

"And the screaming?" Nancy pressed.

"I usually scream when the power goes out," Jane said. "It can be startling, especially if it's night and the lights go off."

"The screams were before the power went out, just before. And the phone call?" Nancy held up her call list. "That's definitely your number that called me!"

"Fine, *that's* a bit weird but it must just be a glitch somewhere. Have you called down to Trevor?"

"Not yet, I didn't know if we should check on anyone else?"

"Why?" Jane asked. "Seriously, I'm sure they're all asleep or are big enough to handle a little power cut."

"Number 86 are awake because they have a visitor; he didn't arrive long ago. Maybe that's where the screaming came from."

Short Horror Stories Volume 3

"Hmm, you don't know who lives there, you said the guy in black was creepy, and you think maybe someone was, what, hurt in there? Just let Trevor deal with it."

"Fine," Nancy said, dialling the concierge's number. "Voicemail," she huffed.

"Just text him, that's what I do if I need something. He's probably busy getting the power back on."

Hi Trevor, it's Nancy from 81. There was some screaming coming from 86, I think. I don't know them so would you mind checking? Thanks.

A moment passed before the phone rang again, the vibrations making both women jump. "It's Trevor," Nancy said, swiping to answer. Once again, the sound of agony-filled screaming came blaring from the tiny speakers and Nancy held the phone at arm's length. Jane could hear it just as well and mouthed a 'what the fuck?', eyes wide. Nancy ended the call and looked at Jane. "That's what happened when you called me too."

"Yeah, that's fucking creepy. Maybe stay here tonight and we'll have a look around when the power comes on." Jane paced about the small living room, glancing outside at the deserted streets. "It's weirdly quiet out there. What time is it?"

"Just gone twelve," Nancy said, checking her phone. "I left my door open. I'll lock up and grab some wine if you want?"

"Want me to come with you?" Jane replied, grinning.

P.J. Blakey-Novis

If Nancy had been honest then she would have given a resounding 'yes', but she tried her best to cover her fear. "It's two doors along, I'm sure I'll be fine."

Jane opened the door to her flat, keeping it wedged in place with her foot, watching as Nancy returned to her own home. She saw Nancy take a step inside. She jumped as the scream rang out, this time coming straight from number 81. Flicking the catch on the door, Jane ran the few metres to Nancy's doorway, looking over her friend's shoulder into the living room. It wasn't dark in there. Shadows danced across the walls and ceiling from countless flickering candles. They were everywhere - on every surface, standing on the carpet, along the windowsill.

In the centre of the room, on top of Nancy's coffee table, sat a small boy all in black. Legs crossed, head in hands, yet frighteningly familiar. Even after Nancy's scream, the child had not moved. Heart thumping, she took a step forward.

"Hello?"

Nothing.

"Did you light these candles?" Jane whispered to Nancy, staying one step behind.

She shook her head. "Hello?" Nancy called out again.

The child's head turned, suddenly, almost bird-like, in their direction. Jane let out a startled gasp. "Charlie?" she whispered. Nancy was about to speak when the child slowly pulled its hands away from its face.

Short Horror Stories Volume 3

Time seemed to slow as the image before them hit home. *The eyes!* They weren't missing, as Nancy had first thought, but were pure, obsidian black. And big. Bigger than any human eyes should be. The women took a step back simultaneously, then another, as the child's mouth widened, not in a sinister grin but in a scream. From its apparently young mouth came the tortured sound of a thousand voices, deafening, angry. Nancy grabbed Jane and ran.

Jane darted into her own flat, into the small room where Charlie still lay fast asleep. Nancy appeared behind her, breathing a sigh of relief that the boy was safe. "It looked just like him," Jane said, fighting back tears.

"I know, but it wasn't."

"So, what now?" Jane asked.

"Police, I guess, but I'm not keen on using my phone." Nancy tried to call Trevor again, and the police, and the hospital. No answer to any of the calls, but her phone would ring soon after and the screams would fill Jane's living room once more.

"Then we need to leave," Jane stated, standing from the sofa. "The lifts will be out of action, so it'll have to be the stairs." It was the only logical thing to do but something pulled at Nancy.

"You're right, but I want to know everyone else is okay. Let's give the others a knock before we make a run for it."

"It's almost one in the morning," Jane replied.

P.J. Blakey-Novis

"I know, but this is kind of an emergency."

Reluctantly leaving Charlie to sleep, they banged on 82, not caring if they upset Maureen and Edgar, but got no reply. They hammered at 84 and 85, certain that all those blood-curdling screams must have woken somebody but, again, no response. Without any real thought, Jane thumped on the last door - apartment number 86. The pair heard movement inside, hushed voices, a weird, metallic scraping sound. Jane and Nancy exchanged nervous glances as they heard a lock turn and the chain slide along and jingle free. Breaths held, flashlight casting eerie shadows, the women waited. The door opened silently, and they found themselves facing a girl in her late teens, wearing a black dressing gown.

"Oh, hi," Jane said, taken aback by the apparent normality of the occupant.

"Have you lost a child?" Nancy interjected, struggling for the right words. "I mean, there's one in my flat. And there's been a lot of screaming. Something weird is going on."

"I haven't heard anything," the girl replied.

"Are your parents home?" Nancy asked, now even more suspicious of the man who had been visiting.

"My dad's here," the girl replied with a shrug. "Dad!"

Appearing from the darkness was the man Nancy had met at the entrance. Something was wrong with this situation just as much as the mess in her flat. "He's your dad?"

Short Horror Stories Volume 3

Nancy asked. "And he's come to visit you?"

"Go back inside, Dorothy," the man ordered, and the girl disappeared into the darkness beyond.

"Good evening ladies, how can I help you? It's rather late to be banging on doors, don't you think?"

"Seriously?" Jane retorted, now finding herself becoming agitated. "There has been screaming going on for the last hour or more, the power is out, there's a weird fucking child in my friend's apartment with candles all over the place, and now we find out people live in number 86. I don't care what time it is; I want to know what's happening."

"And what makes you think I know any more than you do? I'm simply visiting my daughter. Her mother is...away at the moment."

"Look," Nancy began, more than a little afraid of the man. "We didn't want to disturb you, we just wanted to check on each of the neighbours, make sure everybody was okay. There's been no reply at the other flats."

Before the man could respond, a high-pitched whizz filled the air, followed by another, and another. Outside was illuminated by a shower of fireworks, the bright blasts filtering through the windows of apartment 86.

"Fucking kids," Jane muttered, her eyes drawn to the interior of Dorothy's flat which was now lit up by flashes of red, blue, and green. Nancy also looked in that direction but

48

P.J. Blakey-Novis

the man in the black hat stared only forward. For the second time that night, the seconds seemed to slow. The women realised what was before them at the same instant the man knew they had seen it. Each flash of a firework reflected off the blood which soaked the walls, the furniture, even the ceiling. Dorothy stood naked in the middle of the gruesome carnage.

"Well, this is a little awkward," the man said with a smirk. "You are going to need to come inside, I'm afraid." The women took a few steps back, mentally planning to grab Charlie and make a run for the stairs. "INSIDE! NOW!" As he shouted these words his voice grew deeper, otherworldly, almost. The blast of fireworks continued to boom from outside Castle Heights. Nancy moved her head at the sound of a lock being turned, followed by another, and another. A wave of relief washed over her as three doors opened simultaneously. Herbert, Maureen, Edgar, and the two men from 84 all stepped into the corridor.

Nancy shone her phone along the hallway, about to scream for help, when she felt the bile rise to her mouth. Five of her neighbours were facing her, each with eyes as black as the child in her apartment, mumbling something distinctively Latin in origin. They began to shuffle towards her as though in a daze and her mind connected the sight with a familiar zombie series on the television. Turning quickly, she grabbed a hold of Jane's

49

Short Horror Stories Volume 3

arm, yanking her towards the open door of her flat.

"Run!" Nancy yelled, not pausing to wonder why Jane had not said anything. She tried to move her friend but found that she couldn't. Within seconds Nancy felt hands on her neck, Jane's hands, and screamed as she looked into those black orbs. The others were on her in seconds, the narrow corridor giving little room for escape, and Nancy knew she was finished as her neighbours shoved her into apartment 86 and closed the door, darkness falling over her.

Nancy came around to find herself strapped to a chair in a living room very similar to her own. Streetlights provided enough illumination through the bare windows to allow her to make out the basics of her surroundings, to see the man, or monster, perhaps, standing in one corner and puffing on a cigarillo. Nancy could see Dorothy, sitting on the floor in front of the chair, still naked and drenched in blood. The amount of blood was concerning, but that was not the extent of the horror - various chunks of skin, internal organs, and unidentifiable body parts lay scattered about the room. Even as a medical professional, Nancy couldn't tell if these were the remains of one corpse or more.

"What's going on?" Nancy asked. It seemed the most logical question, after all. Maybe an explanation would help but she held onto no

P.J. Blakey-Novis

fantasies of surviving this nightmare.

"Well," began the man, "it's all got a bit messy, I'm afraid. I should have taken more care, I suppose. Dorothy here had said everyone would be asleep." With this last sentence he gave the girl a sharp look, causing her to hang her head.

"Whose blood is this?" Nancy asked, not really wanting to know.

"Nobody important," the man replied. "It was just an offering. That's right, isn't it, Dorothy?"

The girl nodded her head.

"An offering to what?" Nancy said, hardly believing what she was hearing.

"To *whom*, not *what*," the man corrected. "And if you're that interested, it was an offering to *me*."

Nancy looked around the room as well as her restraints would allow, trying to assess the situation. Then she laughed, uncontrollably and hard.

"Because you're what, exactly? A demon? The Devil himself?" Despite everything Nancy had seen over the past few hours, she still had confidence in there being a logical explanation.

"Dorothy summoned me. She had some...shall we say...parenting issues? And to answer your question, I'm clearly not the Devil. I just work for the guy."

"Here's what I think," Nancy said, summoning an unexpected amount of courage and looking directly at Dorothy. "I

Short Horror Stories Volume 3

think you're a little goth kid who got a bit carried away, hated your parents even though they were probably just looking out for you, and, maybe online, you found this fucking joker. Then he tells you to kill them and he'll come to help you. And by help, I assume you've had to fuck him?"

"That's gross," Dorothy replied. "And that's not at all what happened. You wouldn't understand."

"Gross?" the man interjected, feigning his feelings being hurt. "Thank you so much! And no, Nancy, that isn't quite right. Yes, Dorothy here wanted away with her parents. They were scumbags - I won't go into details as it displeases even us denizens of Hell, but she was subjected to things not at all appropriate for children. Yes, she found out about the ritual online, but isn't that how we learn anything nowadays? I may be what you'd call a *bad boy,* but I have certainly not taken advantage of Dorothy. She killed her mother with a knife to the throat while she was passed out drunk, said the right words, and that's when I appeared. Where we first met, in fact, downstairs. It seems so long ago now," he said, wistfully.

"Right, you appeared *downstairs*. Not here, in the flat? And as a demon, you still struggled to get into the building? Righto..." Nancy said.

"DON'T DOUBT MY POWER!" the man yelled, his eyes flickering red, silencing Nancy for a moment.

P.J. Blakey-Novis

"What about her father?" Nancy asked.

"Oh, that was all me!" the man said proudly, his mood switching in a split-second. "I hacked that fucker from anus to mouth and threw his insides about the place. And just to clarify, I never told Dorothy to take her clothes off, that was all her."

"What about the others? That kid in my flat...my neighbours?"

"What about them? The other residents of this delightful building are back in bed - they won't remember a thing. And that child, well, he's with me. He's still in training, I just put him places to scare people. Seems to be effective. Any other questions before we begin?"

"Begin?" Nancy repeated.

"Well, how did you think this would move forward? I'd wipe your mind and put you back to bed?" he asked with a laugh.

"Can you do that?" Nancy said, suddenly hopeful.

"Of course I can! But I won't. I'm afraid your time has come."

Nancy heard a mumbling from Dorothy and tried to listen. More words came, but it was just a whisper. "What are you saying?"

Dorothy looked up, turning to face the creature in the black hat. "You don't have to hurt her. She was trying to help."

"You're right, of course. Thank you. I don't *have* to hurt her. However, I *want* to hurt her. It's in my nature, you see. You summoned me, and this is what you get."

53

Short Horror Stories Volume 3

The demon's hands pointed at Nancy and she felt a pressure building in her ankles. She couldn't see her feet due to them being tied under the chair, but she certainly heard the crack as each ankle broke, the feet now pointing inwards. That same pressure built up in her wrists next, bones breaking, hands hanging limply. Nancy tried to scream but her voice gave out, black spots filling her vision, her mind close to shutting down with shock and pain. Dorothy screamed but it was too late for her to help. Nancy felt each one of her ribs crack, one after another, sharp bone slicing through internal organs. As her mouth filled with blood, Nancy passed out, never to wake.

Jane was awoken by a racket outside Castle Heights soon after 3.30am. The sound of a military helicopter pounded overhead and, dragging herself to her bedroom window, she was shocked to see dozens of uniformed men surrounding the building. She reached for her bedside lamp, finding that the power was off.

"Nancy," she muttered, trying to discern between what had been real and what was a dream. She thought she remembered Nancy coming round, having wine, maybe, and talking to new neighbours. Were they new? She couldn't remember. Jane made her way to her son's room to find him sleeping, then went to use the bathroom. Deciding that the fuzzy memories in her head were just blurry

54

P.J. Blakey-Novis

remnants of a wild dream, she was about to get back into bed.

The silence of the hallway was obliterated by a door swinging open and heavy boots running along the worn carpet. She heard banging on doors, including her own, and grabbed a dressing gown. Opening her front door, she saw each of her neighbours standing in nightwear, looking panicked. All except Nancy. Jane's eyes darted from one end of the corridor to the other as the soldiers entered both flats 81 and 86. There was yelling, words which were hard to make out, before two uniformed men ran from number 86 and vomited on the carpet.

"Everyone back inside! Nobody leaves," someone shouted, prompting each of the residents to return to their flats. Jane waited on her sofa for news, for some explanation as to what was going on, but nothing was coming. The official story she'd read in the papers a few days later: Couple Die from Drug Overdose at Castle Heights, Leaving Only Daughter.

As for Nancy, she must have decided to move on. Some of her clothes were missing and there was a note, after all. Jane couldn't be sure what had happened, everything was still so hazy. But things were looking up and Jane had a reason to be happy - she had a date lined up with one of her neighbours, a handsome man in a black suit from number 86.

Short Horror Stories Volume 3

The Pioneer

I always knew they were out there. I think that most of us did. It seemed pretty unlikely that we'd be alone in the universe, but it still felt like fantasy to actually make contact. I'd always held out some hope that, should we ever encounter a species from beyond the stars, they would be friendly. Surely, we would have a wealth of knowledge to learn from one another? Maybe we could even create a trade agreement with these other beings, something mutually beneficial. Perhaps I was too optimistic in those days. Maybe the thought of war with an alien race was too terrifying to contemplate. The reality, however, was far worse.

It was the year 2130 and I'd been working the lowly role of ship's cook aboard the Starship Pioneer for almost twenty Earth years. The vessel was a research ship primarily, staffed by a team of scientists with a crew of medics, engineers, soldiers, navigators, cooks, and cleaners to support them. Despite being heavily funded by a multi-country initiative, the Pioneer was never expected to return to Earth. The technology was in place to transmit any discoveries back to the command centre, and all aboard fully accepted that this was not a return voyage.

The Pioneer was the fastest and most well-

P.J. Blakey-Novis

equipped vessel ever created. It was capable of travelling further than humankind had ever gone before and, despite a lengthy list of subjects to study, there was always that one underlying goal - to prove the existence of extra-terrestrial life, even make contact with it. In 2111, when we had first set off, there was an excited buzz aboard The Pioneer. The belief that the scientists would succeed in their mission was strong, but it came with a nervousness. There was no guarantee what obstacles we would face or what danger we could be heading into. The presence of the small team of soldiers should have been a comfort but it had the opposite effect on me. Guns in space were a stupid idea and I saw these men as just trigger-happy grunts, more likely to start a conflict than prevent one. Almost twenty years on and they had let themselves go to the point that they wouldn't be much use against an attack anyway.

The time had taken its toll on the majority of the crew, myself included. Boredom had set in much earlier than I had anticipated. The first few years involved a group of us working our way through the hundreds of books and movies stored in the library, playing each and every board game multiple times, and even sharing beds with one another simply for something to do. Most of us were single, or we wouldn't have agreed to a one-way trip into space, and those few that were married when we left knew there was no point keeping those vows now.

Short Horror Stories Volume 3

After a few more years it seemed as though everyone had had enough of each other, or at least had run out of things to talk about. People barely spoke, taking care of their jobs in silence, running on autopilot. Fights would break out on occasion as the pressure of being trapped aboard this metal coffin became too much. Two of the crew took their own lives. Excitement and a sense of adventure had been replaced with a feeling of hopelessness, and the low mood was contagious. Even new discoveries that the scientists made, while interesting to begin with, soon lost their appeal. So what if they had discovered a new element within a piece of space rock? Who cares that their equipment picked up traces of water in a planet's atmosphere? Twenty years ago, those discoveries would have been huge. Now, even the researchers didn't seem to care.

This attitude changed in 2030. This discovery got everyone's attention, tearing apart the boredom and filling The Pioneer with something else. Excitement? Nervousness? Fear? You see, I'm not a scientific man. Although I understand the possible implications of discovering water on an alien planet, that in itself doesn't excite me. However, when the research team called an emergency meeting of all personnel, they had something far more interesting to say.

I had switched off the cooker that I'd be slaving over for the past few hours and shuffled along the brightly lit corridors to the meeting room. The room was designed to accommodate all of the crew at one time, but it still felt crowded, perhaps because we had not all been in there together for more than a year. I thought I'd have to feign interest as Reynolds, the lead researcher, began to speak, but the look on his face piqued my curiosity.

Sweat coated the man's forehead and he dabbed at it with a handkerchief. Glancing nervously at the rest of his team, Reynolds cleared his throat. He hadn't aged well, and I briefly thought back to when I first met the man. He must have been on the wrong side of sixty when we left, putting him into his mid-eighties by now. I remember thinking it was optimistic of them to send someone of his age on such a long mission and was thankful that the rest of his team were at least thirty years his junior.

Reynolds tried to speak but the words were drowned out by the murmurs of the crew and I watched as Veronica, his pretty-in-a-nerdy-way assistant pulled a microphone from one of the cupboards and set it up for him. After a piercing screech of feedback, Reynolds managed to get everyone's attention.

"Good afternoon, ladies and gentlemen," he began, his voice quivering with a combination of nerves and age. "As you may have guessed, we have made a discovery of sorts." I glanced around the faces of the crew, most displaying little to no interest, some even conveying annoyance at having been dragged to this

Short Horror Stories Volume 3

meeting.

"I hope it's better than some new type of rock," one of the cleaning crew piped up. There were a few laughs and nods of agreement.

"I don't know if I'd say it's better," Reynolds replied. "But it could certainly be more interesting." The room fell silent as Reynolds continued. "A few hours ago, Mr Stevenson, our chief navigator, spotted something unusual on the radars. Typically, this far into deep space, we only expect to see rocks and comets, and those are few and far between. What Mr Stevenson spotted is something...else." No one spoke, the crowd seeming to hold in a breath at the same time. "Upon closer inspection, we saw that it was a piece of space junk, similar to the pieces of rockets or satellites which become damaged and float off into space."

"So, it's a bit of rubbish? There have been bits of junk floating around the Earth for well over a hundred years. Could it not have floated out here with a hundred years head start?" one of the soldiers asked.

"No," Reynolds replied, and I'm sure he was trying not to roll his eyes. "We are way too far from Earth for it to be man-made. Which, of course, begs the question - where did it come from?"

"What's the plan, then?" the soldier continued. "I assume you want to bring it aboard?"

"I most certainly do," Reynolds replied. "A

P.J. Blakey-Novis

few of my team, however, have some reservations, so we thought it only fair to explain things in a bit more detail. Veronica, would you mind sharing your concerns?"

Veronica pushed her chair back, causing an uncomfortable scraping sound to echo around the hall. She seemed to mutter a *sorry* before taking the microphone from Reynolds.

"Hi everyone," she began, her nervousness evident. Whether this was related to the discovery or speaking in front of a large crowd I couldn't tell. "So, the item that has come to our attention appears to be around six feet in length, two feet in width, and cylindrical in shape. We have attempted to use our scanning equipment to see inside the item but have had no luck; it appears that the outer material is simply too thick. We have also attempted to scan it for a heat signature but there was not one. These are the standard procedures to determine whether something could be living within this item. Essentially, we've been unable to get a definite answer. There could be nothing in it..."

"Or it could be full of little green men, and we wouldn't know until they were on the ship," the soldier stated.

"In simple terms, you are correct," Reynolds replied to the soldier, taking the microphone from Veronica. "But we have procedures in place for this kind of, erm, event. The capsule would be brought aboard

Short Horror Stories Volume 3

and placed in the isolation chamber. We could then carry out a wide range of tests from inside the laboratory, with no need for anyone to come into contact with it until we were certain it was safe to do so. Of course, our security team would be there to assist, so I'm sure we'll all be perfectly safe." The soldier nodded, looking to the rest of his team for confirmation.

"It's what we're here for," the soldier stated. "Just let us know what you need."

"Do the rest of us get a say in this?" shouted the cleaner. "I mean, if your own team are scared of that thing then are we at least putting it to a vote?" The question was greeted with nodding heads and murmurs of agreement.

"There will be a vote," Veronica interjected. "But not an individual one, as that would take too long. We want the heads of each department to have their say so could those people stay, and everyone else can return to your stations." This approach didn't seem to go down well with a few people, but on the whole I felt relieved not to have the responsibility of making a decision such as this. I returned to the kitchen and awaited the outcome of the discussion I was not deemed important enough to be a part of.

Despite the decision not being unanimous, the majority agreed that the discovery was too important to not investigate further. Reynolds had been vocal in reminding

P.J. Blakey-Novis

everyone that, should the capsule contain alien life, this had been their main goal when they left Earth and it would mean wasting all these years if they ignored this development simply out of fear. For the first time in a long time, The Pioneer was buzzing with chatter and speculation. The lower ranking crew members, such as myself, relied on gossip which had filtered down the chain to keep us updated as events unfolded.

The capsule was brought through to the isolation chamber, so the main hall and rec rooms were much quieter in the evenings as the cleaners, cooks, and engineers spent their time staring at that metal tube through the viewing windows. Talk from inside the laboratory suggested that the scientists had been unable to identify the material and were still unable to ascertain the contents of the capsule. Word came three days later that they were going to attempt to open it; fortunately for me it was my day off and I couldn't resist going to watch their efforts - it wasn't as though I had anything else to do, anyway. I grabbed a coffee from the self-service machine in the canteen just as Veronica was making herself a tea.

"They're opening that thing up today, then?" I asked, trying to make conversation.

"Yep," she replied, the worry on her face unmistakable.

"You don't think it's a good idea?" I asked, walking beside her as she headed back to the lab.

Short Horror Stories Volume 3

"From a scientific point of view, it's absolutely the right thing to do. From a human perspective, it just doesn't feel safe. I mean, it could well be empty, but if it isn't...we have no way of knowing what will be in there and what it could be capable of." I nodded my understanding.

"I'm going to hang out and watch, if that's okay?" I said, knowing that no-one could tell me I couldn't watch from the viewing area. "It's my day off," I added, feeling as though I needed to justify why I was out of the kitchen. Veronica just nodded before she tapped her key-card against the door to the lab and disappeared inside.

The attempts to open the capsule were far less interesting than I had hoped for. I watched Reynolds approach it with three different pieces of equipment, all emitting a high-intensity laser of a different colour, none of which left even a scratch on the shiny surface. Disgruntled and almost crying with frustration, Reynolds called it a night and closed down the lab, plunging the isolation chamber into darkness. I was awoken from my sleep a little after midnight when the sirens began to ring. Every corridor on The Pioneer was illuminated with a red flashing light as I climbed out of bed and opened the door to my small cabin. People ran back and forth in confusion before two soldiers appeared, urging everyone to return to their living quarters and lock the doors. Screams came from the far end of the corridor and I

P.J. Blakey-Novis

hesitated. My eyes flitted between the perceived safety of my room to the sounds of terror not so far away and I made a choice. Perhaps I could help, or perhaps I would die, but at least it wouldn't be boring.

I walked the corridor slowly, trying my best to assess the upcoming situation. It was difficult to identify any other sounds over the blare of the sirens and the screams of the crew but there was something else...a snapping sound, like bones breaking. I passed the laboratory, and the viewing area for the isolation chamber, and stopped in my tracks. The capsule was no longer sealed; an impossibly dark opening had appeared in the top and I stared at it as the red flashes of the warning lights dragged it from the darkness, a second at a time.

I rounded the corner and slipped, falling to the floor. Everything was red, the lights, the floor, the walls. My feet were coated in the blood of someone, but it was now impossible to tell who they had been. Pieces of flesh were scattered about the corridor alongside torn lab coats and crimson ID badges. The walls were covered in blood spatter and there was even some on the ceiling. Veronica had been right to be afraid of that thing.

Just as I was about to make a run for my cabin, a series of three small flashes accompanied the sound of gunfire nearby, followed by an ear-splitting howl. The soldiers were nearby and, thankfully, seemed to be doing their job. Had they killed whatever had

Short Horror Stories Volume 3

come aboard? I ventured onward, keeping my eyes focused on the next turn in the corridor and away from the mess of body parts which littered the ground. Another gunshot, another howl. The creature was still alive, but it was hurt, at least.

I turned the corner as I heard a sickening crunch. One of the soldiers, the last soldier as I quickly discovered, was facing me, his feet dangling a foot off the ground. Holding him in place was what looked like the claw of a scorpion, only much larger, of course. It had pierced his chest from behind and was protruding from the front. I strained in the flashing red lighting to see more details but could not take my eyes from the dying man's face, his mouth gurgling blood, his arms twitching in surrender.

It was not until the creature let the soldier slide from the appendage that I could see what we were facing. I almost let out the most inappropriate of laughs as I surveyed the being that had caused so much destruction, for it looked like an overgrown mantis. It's large, almost perfectly triangular head featured bulbous eyes. Its body was thin but appeared to be entirely made of muscle, supported by strong legs which were as long as the creature was tall. For 'arms' it had the deadly claws which were surprisingly similar to those of a scorpion; sharp, powerful, almost indestructible.

Between the flashes of red light, the creature could not be seen for the blackness

P.J. Blakey-Novis

of its exoskeleton was darker than anything I had ever seen. Even when it was illuminated for those brief moments, it was as if it were merely a shadow of a monster, standing among the debris of humankind. If the armed security team could not destroy this beast then the whole ship was doomed, of that I had no doubt, but I still didn't want to go willingly to my death. I ran, or at least I tried to. The floor was slick with the gruesome remains of my fellow travellers and I fell to the floor numerous times. I refused to look at whatever mess my hands landed in each time I hit the floor, choosing to concentrate on keeping ahead of the creature and the awful clicking sound it made.

Soaked in blood which was, thankfully, not my own, I came to a skid at the entrance to the meeting room. I tried the handle, finding it locked, as the clicking sound grew closer. I watched in terror as the two claw-like appendages appeared from around the corner, quickly followed by the rest of that abomination. It was no more than six feet away from me when I felt a hand grab me by the arm and yank me forward.

Veronica had seen me approach the meeting room in which she had been hiding out with another of the science team - a man a little older than me and well within the category of morbidly obese. She had taken a risk by unlocking the door and pulling me to safety, albeit temporary safety, and her colleague was clearly angered by my

Short Horror Stories Volume 3

presence. He explained in hissed whispers how stupid Veronica had been, how it was now every man for himself, and so on. I thought, but had the decency not to say, that if the three of us were to be chased then this chap would make our escape much easier, not to mention keeping that thing fed for some time.

"It seems you were right," I whispered to Veronica.

"I wish I hadn't been," she told me, her eyes tearing up. "Is there anyone else out there?"

"I don't know," I replied. "Lots of people were locking themselves in their cabins, but the soldiers are all dead. They wounded that creature, but it's still fast. It's pretty horrific up by the lab."

"So, what are we supposed to do?" asked the big guy. "If we can't kill it then we're all going to die! We need to get guns."

"If you feel like going back out there and searching for guns, in the dark, among the leftover pieces of the soldiers, you go ahead," I said, knowing it would be suicide.

"Funny," he replied. "I think I'd rather we go to the ammo room." Veronica and I looked at each other in confusion.

"I thought the soldiers only carried a handgun each, so as not to run the risks that come with having a whole arsenal on a bloody spaceship!" Veronica said.

"You really think they only had a few handguns? I heard them talking before about

P.J. Blakey-Novis

some high-tech bullets for some new rifles. One of the guys was complaining that they couldn't test them out."

"How come they didn't have them tonight?" I asked. "If they had better weapons, why not actually use them when they were needed?"

"He's talking shit," Veronica said. "Our best chance is to stay here and keep out of sight."

"Until when?" her colleague demanded. "Until we starve? Until we're the last ones left, and we just wait for a fucking alien to break in and kill us? We have to try something." And, for the first time, I had to agree with the guy.

"He's right," I said, looking at Veronica as best I could in the darkness. "But I'll go. You're safer in here for now, and you..." I paused as I turned to face the huge man, "...you'll slow me down. Just tell me where this ammo store is." He didn't even try to go with me, and I wondered if sending me had been his plan all along.

"When I say ammo room, it's more of a cupboard than a room, I think. I've never actually seen it. I just heard the guys talking about it a while ago. But I'm sure it's near the soldiers' quarters, and it won't say what it is on the door."

"Helpful," I replied, approaching the exit to the meeting room. I pressed my ear against the door, listening for any more of that awful clicking but heard nothing. In my head I planned my route, knowing that my best

Short Horror Stories Volume 3

chance for survival was to get there quickly and locked into the ammo room. If the creature followed then so be it, at least I'd be armed. *Open the door, run to the left, past my cabin and on to the lift, down one level, follow the corridor to the right.* I'd only been past the soldier's quarters once before and had laughed at how overly macho it had been. The rest of The Pioneer was immaculate but those few cabins had been decorated like a teenage boy's bedroom, with posters of topless women holding ridiculously large guns, sports cars, and military vehicles. I racked my brain to locate any other rooms along there but came up short. *Only one way to find out.*

I gave Veronica a curt nod as I gently opened the door, holding my breath as it let out a small creak. No sound aside from the blare of the alarm could be heard so I stepped into the corridor. I glanced around, took a deep breath, and ran as fast as I could. The carnage was far less in this direction, leading me to believe that the monster had headed back to where I had met it, presumably to feast on what flesh remained.

I reached the lift safely, hitting the call button and staring into the darkness from whence I had come, expecting to see claws emerge from the shadows. Nothing came for me, not even the lift, which I presumed was a safety protocol triggered by the alarm sounding. The stairwell was only a few feet

P.J. Blakey-Novis

further, so I reached it in a matter of seconds and began to descend the metal steps, my shoes clanging against them noisily. One floor meant eighteen steps in two sections of nine and, when I reached the level I needed, a thought hit me. The shape of the creature's legs and its overall size made me question its ability to follow me down here. Perhaps that thing could be contained to one floor, at least for now.

I hurried along, checking each door that I passed. Each of the soldiers' cabins were unlocked and uninhabited. At the far end, as the corridor turned to the right, there were two more doors. One was labelled as a cleaner's stockroom, presumably for mops, cleaning products, cloths, and the like. The other just carried a warning of high voltage and a clear *Keep Out* sign. With no doubt in my mind, I pulled at the door, but it refused to budge. *Of course it'd be locked up securely,* I thought, hardly daring to consider where the key would be kept. *If it's not in the security chief's room, then it must have been on his person and that's as good as lost.*

I quickly made my way through the cabins, trying to discover which belonged to the Chief of Security. I never found out which room was his, just as I never discovered the whereabouts of the key, and I never found out if that door really did lead to an ammo supply. So many unanswered questions. The one question that I now *did* have an answer to related to the creature's ability to

Short Horror Stories Volume 3

manoeuvre itself down stairs. It stood at the foot of the stairwell, its impossible blackness a silhouette of terror in the dark, building up to a crescendo of clicking. I could try to run, but what was the point? We weren't getting into the weapons stash, we couldn't isolate this thing on one floor and just carry on our existence as though it wasn't there. For all I knew, I was the last human left on The Pioneer. Fear turned to relief as I faced that thing head on. I knew it was futile, but I no longer cared. That monster, that alien, brought with it an end to the boredom. Even so, I managed a smile at the knowledge we had succeeded in our mission, even if that success was not quite as everyone had hoped. We had discovered the existence of extra-terrestrial life and I'm sure that Reynolds, especially at his age, died a happy man with this knowledge.

I charged at the creature, intending to land blows on its bony exoskeleton but I never made it that far. It stuck out one clawed limb just as I got close enough and I felt it glide through my chest and tear free from my back. I felt, more than heard, the crack of my ribs as they shattered, and felt myself choking on the warm, metallic blood which now flowed freely. I looked into the creature's eyes as it tilted its head, appearing to examine me, and then nothing but darkness.

P.J. Blakey-Novis

The Tom Booker Sessions

Patient ID: 140796 - Tom Booker
Session 1: April 14th, 2020

"Why don't we start at the beginning?" Doctor Nicola Matthews suggested. She gazed at Tom through thick-rimmed glasses, her eyes seeming to flow with genuine sadness for his current state. Any other person would have noticed how stunning this woman was but not Tom, his eyes darted nervously around the room, verifying the safety of the place. Tom was new to therapy, despite having known it was needed for most of his life, and he was already onto his third doctor. But Nicola felt right, or as right as any therapist could feel. Not only had she removed any mirrors from the room, she had also taken down frames from the wall. Tom could just make out the slight change in colour where they had hung, certificates, he presumed. The waiting room had appeared just as ready for his arrival and, to Tom, this demonstrated a deep understanding of his issue.

"Tom?" Nicola pressed. Tom kept his gaze fixed on the patterns in the carpet, red and orange swirls which his eyes followed endlessly, until he mumbled something. "I didn't catch that, Tom," Nicola said.

Tom raised his head a little. "Could you

Short Horror Stories Volume 3

take your glasses off?" he said, awkwardly, his eyes now reaching the doctor's shoes. There was a pause, followed by the sound of the frames being placed on a side table.

"I'm sorry," Nicola said. "I hadn't thought of that. I may need them on to make some notes, but I'll warn you first, okay?" Tom nodded, his gaze moving up across the black trousers, the white blouse, and finally on to the doctor's face. "So, the beginning? I have some notes from your previous doctor. It mentions an accident when you were four?" Tom nodded, trying as hard as he could to keep focused on the doctor when she spoke. "A car accident? What can you tell me about that?"

Tom took a deep breath to steel himself. He had known this would need to be discussed, he knew it was an essential part of the recovery he was so desperate to make, but the words felt too heavy to force from his mouth.

"Take your time," Nicola said, her expression warm.

"Erm," Tom began, letting out a small cough. "We were on our way to somewhere, a zoo I think my aunt said, and a truck jumped a red light. I only really know what I was told later. Our car was hit on the driver's side, my dad was killed instantly. I was in a car seat behind my mum. We got flipped over. She died too."

"And do you have any memory of the crash yourself?" Nicola asked.

P.J. Blakey-Novis

This was the very question which had brought his sessions with the previous two therapists to an end. Yes, he did remember something, something which had brought him to this point. Even before he could allow the memory to form in his mind, he felt himself begin to shake. Tom's heart rate increased, droplets of sweat forming on his forehead. This was nothing new and he took a moment to breathe deeply and regain his composure. His one lingering memory of that day almost twenty years previous, was the root cause of everything that he'd been through since.

"I think maybe I was unconscious for a bit, it's all quite hazy. When I opened my eyes, the car was on its side, on the driver's side. It must have rolled right over. I was still strapped into place, I remember that, and there were a lot of people outside the car. Through the gap between the door and the seat in front of me, I could see the side mi... mirror," Tom stuttered, struggling to get the last word out without vomiting. "Through that I could see my mum's face. Her eyes were open but there was bruising around her neck and cheeks. I'm sure she was trying to speak as our eyes met in the reflection but then she was gone. I saw her go." Tom's breathing became deeper as he attempted to quell the panic rising inside, as he tried to focus on the pride he felt at having been able to tell the doctor what he had experienced. Nicola sat quietly and Tom took it as cue to

Short Horror Stories Volume 3

continue. "This problem, either spectrophobia or catoptrophobia, whichever one you want to call it, started then, I'm sure of it."

Tom watched Nicola nodding as she chose her next words. "Tom, would you say it's got worse as you've got older? Your previous therapist describes the condition as severe which is why I took the step of removing any possible triggers from my office. Apologies again for the glasses, I hadn't even considered that."

"I don't know if it's got worse," Tom admitted. "Now that I'm in my own place and have more control, I can avoid some triggers. My aunt tried her best but..." Tom shrugged.

"You lived with your aunt for fifteen years?" Nicola asked, Tom confirming with a nod. "And what can you tell me about those years?"

Tom sat up a little straighter in an attempt to convey a confidence he did not feel. His hands were shaking less than they had been, but he continued to nervously spin the ring on his right thumb. "I couldn't tell you when the first time was, but it must have been soon after the funeral. I'd been in the hospital for several days after the accident and then we buried my parents a week or so after I was released. It's odd really. I don't have many memories from that time, I guess because I was so young, but the ones linked to my, erm, condition, are still vivid."

"So you remember the first time a reflection frightened you? Aside from on the

76

P.J. Blakey-Novis

day of the accident," Nicola asked.

"It was at the funeral," Tom replied with certainty. "Or rather, just after the funeral. My aunt led me to the car which was waiting to take us to the wake; a black town car with tinted windows. I caught a glimpse of my face in the reflection, my aunt standing behind me. Only it wasn't my aunt, it was my mum. Her face was pale and streaked with purplish lines, one eye swollen shut, lips cracked and bloody. I heard my name being called and I could have sworn it was her." Tom's voice had risen several octaves and Nicola saw the fear in him.

"And do you think it was her now, looking back on that experience?"

"Logic tells me it was my aunt's reflection, they were sisters, after all, and that it was her who said my name, probably telling me to get in the car. But it felt so real. Even looking back on it, whenever I feel brave enough to think about it in any detail, which isn't often, I still see it the way I saw it then. And even if that could be explained away, it doesn't account for everything else that's happened since."

As Tom braced himself to continue, he was interrupted by a beeping from the doctor's mobile. She gave him a weak smile and informed him they were out of time for this session. "We'll pick this up next week, Tom. What you have is not very common, but the cause seems easy to determine, which makes treatment quite viable. Next week we'll talk

Short Horror Stories Volume 3

about your other experiences and start putting a plan together to get you well. How does that sound?"

"Good," Tom managed, matching the faint smile of the doctor. Despite the difficult subject matter, Tom was relieved he had managed to say as much as he had, and he left Doctor Matthews' office a little happier than when he had entered.

Patient ID: 140796 - Tom Booker
Session 2: April 21st, 2020

"How are you feeling today, Tom?" Nicola asked. He took a quick look around the room, finding it as it had been on the previous week and managed a smile.

"You remembered about the glasses," he said. "I feel okay, I think. I've been trying to decide what to tell you about today. It all starts to sound quite repetitive."

"How about I ask some questions, then?" the doctor asked. Nicola waited for a nod from Tom before continuing. "These all relate to any time since the day of the accident, okay?" Tom nodded again. "After the incident at the funeral which you told me about last week, roughly how long was it before something similar happened?"

"I don't know," Tom replied. "I mean, I was four. Maybe a week or two?"

"So, you didn't see the image of your mother in every reflective surface?"

"Not then, no. It was maybe once or twice a

78

P.J. Blakey-Novis

month to begin with. Always the same though. Her face always pale and cracked, the same eye always swollen shut, appearing over my right shoulder. Of course, I'd jump at the sight, swing around to find nobody there. Even when I'd turned away from the mirror, or the car door, or even the fucking TV screen, I'd still hear my name being whispered. It would happen whether I was alone or not, so I couldn't put it down to my aunt being behind me."

"And you told your aunt about these...incidents?" Nicola asked, her eyes fixed on Tom's nervously bouncing leg.

"I had to. She'd hear my screaming. I'd often wet myself out of fear. She said I'd often be hysterical."

"And what did she say to reassure you?" Nicola asked, wondering what she herself would tell a four-year-old having visions of his dead mother.

"I don't remember her saying much at all. There were hushed words between my aunt and other family members, but I guess they put it down to trauma. When I started school, they had someone come see me each week, but I didn't like them. They'd take me out of class and make me draw what I'd seen in the mirror. After a couple of years, I pretended it had stopped."

This caught Nicola by surprise and she looked at Tom, her brow furrowed. "You pretended it had stopped? How?"

"By not reacting," Tom stated. "Each day

Short Horror Stories Volume 3

went the same way and I soon learned which surfaces to avoid. Mirrors were the worst, of course, but they can be avoided if you really try. I'd go to the bathroom with my eyes fixed to the ground, I'd avoid looking at cars as they passed me, and eventually I'd only see mum once every few months. Sometimes I'd let out a scream as she would catch me off-guard, but I'd quickly play it down as something else having frightened me. By the time I was seven, my aunt thought it had stopped completely and she never mentioned it again."

"So, just let me make sure I'm following correctly, when was the last time you saw this image of your mother?"

"January 1st," Tom replied.

"Wow, okay," Nicola began. "Almost four months ago. What happened that time to make you so certain of the date?"

"Well," Tom said, his cheeks reddening a little, "I'd met up with some friends on New Year's Eve, at my place, of course. I don't go anywhere that I don't know well, just in case. My friend Brian came with his girlfriend, who also brought a friend. Long story short, the new girl, Martha, stayed at mine that night. In the morning she was making coffee and I walked up behind her to give her a hug." Tom paused, tears beginning to form. "I put my chin on her shoulder and realised she was doing her makeup in a compact mirror and as soon as I saw it, there she was."

"Your mother?"

P.J. Blakey-Novis

"Perhaps. Something that *was* my mother at some point, anyway. I saw the face, same as always, and I must have gripped Martha a little too tightly. She let out a yelp just as I screamed. I don't know if Brian had told her about my, erm, problem, but she was out the door before I could even try to explain. I haven't seen her since."

"And does that worry you?" Nicola asked.

"Of course! Not about Martha in particular, but what kind of relationship could I have with this going on? I just want to be normal." Tom began to break down, unable to fight the sobs that took him over.

"And January was the last time you saw...*her?* Your mother?" Nicola handed a box of tissues to her patient as Tom nodded. "Is this because you've avoided any triggers? Or have the...visions become less frequent?"

"I've dealt with this all my life," Tom mumbled between sobs. "I know how to avoid the things that trigger it. But it's not practical to carry on like this. So, what do we do?" Tom lifted his head from his hands and looked into the doctor's eyes, pleading, desperate.

"Okay," Nicola began, thinking through her answer. "From a therapist's point of view there are a number of steps when dealing with a patient. Firstly, establish what the issue is. In this case, as you know, it's a phobia. The next step is to get to the root of the problem, the incident which caused the phobia to develop. You were already aware of

81

Short Horror Stories Volume 3

the effect your parents' accident had on you. That leaves the most difficult part - treatment. In your case, the phobia is triggered by PTSD. Your mind makes a connection between any reflective surface and you seeing your mother die."

Tom sighed. "That's pretty much what I already knew. I wish I could explain how real it all feels when I see her. But how do I stop her from appearing? I haven't even seen my own face for months!"

"This might sound absurd," Nicola began, "but have you tried talking to your mother?"

Tom looked incredulous. "Talking to a hallucination? That would make me crazier than I already am!"

"I'm not saying she is really there, of course. I just mean that whatever your mind is trying to create could be tricked into some form of closure."

"I'm not following," Tom admitted.

"Sorry. What I mean is that, somewhere in your mind, you still feel as though your mother wants to talk to you. If you allowed yourself to see her again, if you could control the fear you've been feeling, perhaps you could get answers?"

Tom shrugged, torn between wanting the nightmare to be over and feeling terrified at the thought of facing his fear head-on. "What are you suggesting I do?"

"Nothing until next week; just carry on as you have been. We're almost out of time, anyway. I don't want anything to upset you.

P.J. Blakey-Novis

When we have our session next Tuesday, we'll face the mirror together."

Tom's hands began to tremble, his face draining of colour. He'd expected this at some point, but not this quickly. "I'll do my best," he replied, forcing a thin smile.

"That's all you can do," Nicola reassured. "And I'll be right beside you, ready to stop it if it becomes too much."

Patient ID: 140796 - Tom Booker
Session 3: April 28th, 2020

"Good afternoon, Tom," Doctor Matthews began, holding open the sturdy office door for him to enter. Tom's shaking hands were obvious, and he looked as though he hadn't slept since their last session. "How are you feeling about today?"

"Fucking terrified," Tom said, bluntly. "But I'm here."

"I'm glad," Nicola replied. "I know this is difficult, but we can stop whenever you like and I'm right here." The doctor motioned to the armchair which Tom had taken previously. Once Tom was seated, pulling at his fingers with anxiety, Nicola moved to stand behind him. "Now, Tom, I have a mirror with me." The sound of the m-word caused a violent flutter in his stomach. "I'm going to slowly lower it in front of us so I can see in it as well. I need you to remain as calm as possible and tell me what happens."

Tom's hands had moved onto the arms of

Short Horror Stories Volume 3

the chair, knuckles white as his fingers dug in. He managed a small nod and Nicola began lowering the mirror, her forearms coming to rest on her patient's shoulders. The mirror was inches from Tom's face, and he had not reacted.

"Tom," Nicola said quietly. "What can you see?"

"My eyes are closed," he replied. "I'm building up to it."

"Take as long as you need."

Summoning all his courage and determination, Tom opened his right eye, just a crack. It took a fraction of a second before he was able to focus on what was in front of him. The deep brown of the eye was familiar, and his focus flicked towards the reflection of his left eye, still scrunched closed. Pupil darting around the surface of the glass and only finding his own face, Tom gradually opened his left eye.

"What do you see?" Nicola asked.

"It's too close to my face," Tom said. "I can't see anything beyond my eyes and nose." Nicola tilted the mirror to allow Tom to see her standing behind him.

"Tom," she began, but it reached Tom's ears as a whisper. Tom's eyes gazed at the refection of the doctor's blouse, worked their way up to her neck, and then he screamed.

"Tom," Nicola repeated, and Tom saw the reflected mouth move, the bloodied, cracked lips part. Eye swollen shut, pale face riddled with purplish streaks. Tom tried to stand, to

P.J. Blakey-Novis

push past the mirror being held to his face, but something held him in place. The arms which had gently rested on his shoulders now felt like restraints. Tom risked another glance at the abomination in the reflection and saw it smiling, blood dripping from fresh cracks as the lips stretched.

"What do you want?" Tom yelled. Unable to run, Tom chose to take Nicola's advice about facing this nightmare head on. "Tell me what you want!" he said through tears.

"Tom..." the voice said again, the one good eye still staring, that horrific grin continuing to spread.

"Fuck this," Tom muttered, head-butting the mirror and sending it crashing to the floor. Tom chanced a quick glance to ensure it wasn't facing upwards before attempting to stand. The arms remained in place on his shoulders and he strained his head to look at his therapist.

"Doctor Matthews?" Tom whispered. "Sorry, can you let me up?" There was a pause, as though the doctor was processing the request, before he felt the weight lift.

"Sorry Tom," Nicola said. "I'm not sure what came over me." The doctor moved around to her seat, trying to compose herself despite her evident confusion. "What did you see?"

"I saw *her*, the same as I always do." Tom began to cry but they were tears of anger, anger at his failure to resolve the problem coupled with embarrassment at smashing the

Short Horror Stories Volume 3

mirror. "Sorry about your mi... mirror," he mumbled. "I assume you didn't see anything weird?" Tom asked.

"I... erm, no, I didn't. I must have zoned out, I'm sorry. I remember tilting the mirror and then you were trying to get up."

"When I saw her," Tom explained, "she was you. Or you were her, whatever. I looked at the reflection when you tilted it, tried to look at you, but your face wasn't yours."

"I think we need to cut this session short today, if you don't mind?" the doctor said. "I'm feeling a little unwell and you're clearly upset. Perhaps we can try again next week?"

Tom was relieved that Nicola wasn't suggesting they go through that again so soon and quickly made his way out of the office. Doctor Matthews, however, stayed fixed in her chair, unable to move.

April 30th 2020
Police interview with Tom Booker

"Miss Matthews was your therapist?" the scruffy detective asked as Tom fidgeted uncomfortably in the interview-room chair. Tom couldn't look anywhere safely. The table was stainless steel, the tape recorder on that table was a reflective silver, even the linoleum floor seemed to create shadows in his peripheral vision. Tom only managed a nod. "You were the last person to see her alive," the detective explained for the third time since he'd been brought to the station. "Can

P.J. Blakey-Novis

you tell me what you spoke about?"

"I didn't do anything to her," Tom muttered. "She was nice."

"Maybe you didn't, that's what we're trying to determine. But Miss Matthews' cause of death has been ruled asphyxiation and you were the last person there. I'm sure you can see how it looks. Did you notice anyone else waiting to see her? Anyone hanging around outside?"

Tom shook his head. "No," he said.

"How was she when you left her?"

"She said she wasn't feeling well," Tom explained. "We cut the session short."

The detective's face registered a little surprise, but he hid it quickly. "What sort of unwell?"

"She didn't say. We'd had a weird session so hadn't really talked much. I think I'd only been there about twenty minutes."

"Weird how?"

"Do you know why I was seeing her?" Tom asked.

"I'm still waiting on the court to grant access to your file but you're welcome to tell me about your sessions."

"I have spectrophobia," Tom stated. The detective shrugged, waiting for Tom to elaborate. "A fear of m... mi... mirrors. Or seeing things in them. It's so bad that I see her in any shiny surface. You probably noticed I haven't looked at the table?"

"Her?" the detective asked.

"It's a woman, sort of." Tom swallowed

Short Horror Stories Volume 3

hard, knowing that he needed to be as honest as possible with the detective. "But like a corpse. It all stems back to the crash that killed my parents. I saw my mum die, reflected in the wing mirror."

"Okay, so what happened during your last session?"

"Doctor Matthews wanted me to face the phobia. We looked in a mi... mirror together, I saw what I always saw and freaked out, broke the... thing."

"And did the doctor see anything... weird?" the detective asked.

"Of course not," Tom replied. "I know it's in my head. But she seemed a bit confused after and said we should end the session."

"Nothing else?"

"That was it, I was desperate to get out of there," Tom explained.

"Bear with me please," the detective said, making his way out of the room. Muttered voices came from the hallway outside, but Tom could only make out snippets, words like *fake* and *test* and the dreaded m-word. The detective returned with a female officer who assumed a position behind Tom's chair.

"Mr. Booker," the detective began. "Your aunt tells us you had this fear of mirrors as a child, but that it hasn't been a problem for many years. She raised you, yes? She didn't even know you were in therapy."

"She didn't understand, not really. I hid it from her as best I could," Tom said.

"So, there's no diagnosis anywhere? No

88

P.J. Blakey-Novis

evidence that you really have this...spectro...whatever you called it?"

"I'm not following," Tom said, unsure why the police would not believe him.

"Can you prove it?"

"How?!" Tom demanded. "If I look in a m... mirror then I'll see her, but you won't. My reaction could just be staged, for all you know. I wouldn't say there was any way to prove it." The detective gave an almost imperceptible nod over Tom's shoulder to the female officer. Before Tom knew what was happening, a compact mirror was flipped open in front of him. His own distraught face was reflected back at him but there was something else, something which caused him to scream out and thrash against the handcuffs that bound him. Over his shoulder, the face grinned through cracked lips, this time in a police uniform. *Tom*, came the whisper of his name.

The mirror was out of Tom's restricted reach, but he diverted his eyes, moving his gaze to the detective who sat opposite. He sat, slack-jawed, not even looking at Tom. The man stared over Tom's shoulder at the policewoman, as though he could see something terrible there. The mirror moved a little closer, just close enough for Tom to lean forward and grab at it with his teeth. He managed to fling it from the woman's grasp and out of sight.

"Detective?" Tom whispered as the man on the other side of the table continued to stare

Short Horror Stories Volume 3

at something behind Tom. The detective tried to speak, his mouth moving to form words, but nothing came aside from a gurgling sound. His eyes widened, still fixed on whatever horror stood in that room, as his oesophagus began to close. Tom watched in terror as the detective suffocated on what appeared to be nothing, his head crashing onto the table.

The female police officer stepped around Tom and leaned her face into his. Her pale, bruised, cracked face. Tom stared, unable to process what he was seeing, as the officer proceeded to release the handcuffs.

"Tom," she said, barely above a whisper. "We need to go."

"Where?"

"Home, Tom, I'm taking you home. You've been through a lot. It's time to let mummy take care of you."

P.J. Blakey-Novis

Break-In at St. Benedict's

The day of the village fete was not Father Harris's favourite day of the year. In fact, any day that involved having to make small talk with the residents of Sweet Little Chittering was a day he could do without. Sundays were the worst, although he did like to see that the number of parishioners who would attend his weekly service was dwindling. For a village, or more accurately a *hamlet*, of less than five hundred residents, only having the same twenty to thirty worshippers to endure on a Sunday morning wasn't too trying. And almost all of those were so ancient they couldn't really hear him anyway. He could have been reciting the Satanic Verses at the pulpit and they would have nodded along regardless.

It was an odd attitude for a vicar to have, of this he was well aware. Aware, but couldn't care less. He had been placed in this church for almost thirty years with one particular task. The powers above didn't care about the congregation size, or how much loose change was sprinkled onto the donation plates. They just needed him to make sure their secrets were safe. Taking the reins at St Benedict's was a far higher position than anyone (outside of a select few) knew. Having gone into the ministry at the tender age of twenty, Father Harris had an eagerness for the

Short Horror Stories Volume 3

spiritual fight. He had no interest in merely steering his flock on the right path, he wanted exorcisms, miracles, and all the drama that came with a life of battling evil. Now, alone in his office on the morning of the village fete, he found himself longing for some excitement of the spiritual kind.

Stirring a sugar cube into his tea, Father Harris glanced at the clock hanging a little off centre above his desk. 9.45am. The fete was due to open officially at ten and he spent the next few minutes wondering if his absence would be noticed before deciding that he had little option but to show his face. *But when?* he deliberated. *If I go now, I could end up stuck there until this evening. I'd rather not have to sit through those bastard Morris Dancers. Perhaps I can greet everyone and then disappear. Return later for the fireworks.*

Harris decided to go by soon, before it became busy, say a few hellos, and then disappear on 'important Church business'. He'd no doubt have to return at some point, but that could wait until much later in the day when it was dark and easier to remain out of sight. Getting up from his chair with a groan, he picked up the white collar and slipped it into place. The sun was streaming through the stained-glass around him and so he left his jacket draped across the desk. To the right of the small office was a semi-hidden door behind a filing cabinet. It blended into the wall, but the outline could

P.J. Blakey-Novis

be seen if you were really looking. Harris glanced at the door before leaving the office and making his way out of the church. The heavy double doors that made up the main entrance were left open, as was often the case should any lost soul be seeking a place of refuge.

Father Harris took the stroll slowly, enjoying the warmth of the sun and the relative quiet of the area. Fifteen minutes later, the sounds of children (both laughing and screaming), as well as some awful music, filled his ears. He let out a groan but kept walking, mentally preparing a route around the fete and already thinking about lunch. Harris patted the rear pocket in his trousers to confirm his wallet was where it should be as his stomach grumbled. *Could get some food from one of the stallholders,* he mused. *As long as it isn't rock cakes like last year. Tasted like actual bloody rocks.* Harris caught a whiff of food as he stepped onto the village green and it turned his stomach – a greasy, fried onion stench that had to be coming from an out-of-town burger van.

Father Harris glanced about, trying to ascertain who was where so he could plan a route which involved the least conversation. Cautiously, he made his way to the first stall and offered a cheery 'Morning!'. It looked like someone was just trying to shift their old junk so he moved on, greeting each trader while wondering if anyone would actually sell anything. *It's all a load of crap,* he thought.

Short Horror Stories Volume 3

Having made his way around the entire fete, Father Harris had only parted with a few pounds which had gone on two cheese scones and a slice of homemade fudge cake.

It wasn't quite eleven and Harris had intended to take the food back to the quiet of his office, but his stomach suggested otherwise. Taking a seat at a bench to the far end of the green, he hoped for a few solitary moments to enjoy his food. He had taken one bite of a scone when the scent hit his nostrils. *Cannabis,* he decided, his eyes flitting along the edge of the field. He took a second bite as he continued scanning for the culprits and then he saw them, just behind a thick oak tree. Father Harris couldn't tell how many *they* were, but there was faint laughter coming from at least two voices and a feminine leg was visible, stretching out on the grass.

Sweet Little Chittering had a pretty low population of teenagers, so Father Harris could place a fairly safe bet on who that leg belonged to. And if that really was Leanne, then her headmaster father would not be happy with her drug use. *Just teenagers,* Harris thought. *Not hurting anyone.* For a brief moment he considered going over and doing his duty, attempting to steer the youngsters onto the right path. *Futile,* he decided. *Especially at that age.* Halfway through his second scone, however, he found himself forced to engage with the kids.

"I think the priest is enjoying the view!"

P.J. Blakey-Novis

Father Harris looked up to see a seventeen-year-old couple approaching. He glanced back to the leg and, realising he had been staring in that direction, found himself becoming flustered. "Don't be so ridiculous, Tommy," he said, brushing crumbs from his shirt as he stood.

"Hey, Leanne! Old man Harris has been checking you out. I think he might want to take you to church for a baptism. You'll need your bikini." The girl on Tommy's arm, Lizzy, faked a sound like she was about to vomit.

Father Harris felt his face flush red with a mix of anger and embarrassment. *Prick,* he thought, but dared not utter aloud. "Here to enjoy the fete?" he asked instead. "Hope you're all going to be on your best behaviour today."

"Not sure yet," Tommy replied with a grin. "What do you guys think?" he yelled over to Leanne and her younger brother, Jonah, who were approaching from their position behind the tree.

"About what?" Leanne asked.

"Father Harris was asking if we're going to be on our best behaviour today."

"Oh Father, I'm *always* on my best behaviour," Leanne told him. "I've never done anything...*naughty.*"

Harris felt his face redden a little more. "Well, I hope you all enjoy the day. I need to get back to the church, but I'll be around again later, if any of you wish to talk about anything."

Short Horror Stories Volume 3

"Thank you, Father," Leanne replied sweetly as she watched him leave the village green and make his way back towards the church.

Tommy spent the next hour or so leading the group around the fete, looking at stalls and making rude comments to the other villagers. Lizzy laughed as Tommy placed a hand-knitted tea cosy on her head, much to the disapproval of the elderly lady who had created the masterpiece. Leanne and Jonah both felt a twinge of embarrassment at their friends' behaviour but not to the point they would actually leave. Everyone in Sweet Little Chittering knew what Tommy was like, and all secretly waited for the day he would undoubtedly end up in jail. All the villagers could hope was that it wouldn't be for any crime that impacted on them.

"It must be gin o' clock by now," Lizzy decided, looking at Tommy, eyebrows raised. She was putting in an order, that much was clear, and despite his bravado Tommy knew who was really in charge.

"What do you want me to do about it?" he asked. "I can't get served in this shithole. Everyone knows how old I am."

"I didn't say *buy* any," Lizzy replied, waiting for Tommy to catch up with her train of thought.

"Right..." he said slowly. For a moment he looked nervous at the prospect of stealing but quickly buried the feeling, marching towards

96

P.J. Blakey-Novis

the local store.

"Tommy!" she called, catching up with him.

"What?"

"Are you just going to walk in and grab a bottle? We'll need tonic water too..." Lizzy said, now in a whisper. "Take my bag."

Grabbing the cotton tote bag from his girlfriend, Tommy glanced through the store window. Only the clerk could be seen, and Tommy knew he'd be closely watched from the moment he entered. "I know, you two distract him," he suggested, nodding at Lizzy's breasts. "While he's gazing at them, I'll get what I can. Just ask him about something behind the counter."

"Aw, Tommy, you're so sweet. I'm glad my only use is my tits," Lizzy huffed. The desire for alcohol to fuel the day however meant more than a little self-respect and she entered the shop, followed a moment later by Tommy. The clerk was no fool, and while shoplifting in such a small village was rare, Tommy and Lizzy were famously a couple and certainly bad news. For Lizzy to be rather awkwardly thrusting her cleavage in the clerk's face whilst Tommy skulked about with an empty bag wasn't going to fool anyone.

"Out," the clerk ordered, sounding almost bored. Neither teenager felt it was worth protesting innocence and left with a huff.

"No luck?" Leanne asked as the pair joined them outside the shop.

"Nah," Tommy said. "Didn't think it'd work

Short Horror Stories Volume 3

anyway. Guess it'll be a dry one."

"We can't get any gin," Leanne said, "but how about red wine?"

"Yuck," Jonah added.

"Obviously not for you, you're far too young," Leanne added.

"What difference does it make?" Lizzy asked. "If we could get anything, it'd have to be from here." She waved a hand vaguely in the direction of the village store.

"When was the last time you went to church?" Leanne asked.

Tommy and Lizzy laughed, not following at all. "You think we need to go confess our sins for wanting a nab a bottle?" Tommy said with a smirk.

"Sometimes, Tommy, you aren't all that smart. Confession...probably not. But what happens at communion?"

Leanne was right that Tommy was far from being a genius and the same could easily be said for Lizzy. It took a moment, but they seemed to reach the same conclusion at the same time, grins appearing on both their faces.

"The church!" they squealed in unison.

"But what about Harris?" Tommy asked.

"We'll see," Leanne replied, now feeling as though she were leading the group. "The church is open so we can go by, sit inside, and work it out from there. Must be worth a try."

"You go in first," Tommy suggested, looking

P.J. Blakey-Novis

at Leanne. "See if anyone is about." Leanne nodded her head at Jonah, signalling for him to follow, and made her way inside. They paused just inside the main doors, taking a moment for their eyes to adjust to the darkness. The church was ancient and had a distinctive odour, like polished wood and old books. The uncomfortable looking pews sat empty, the only light coming through the stained-glass windows and barely illuminating the space.

Leanne felt Jonah take a step closer. The place was eerily quiet but she told herself that it was supposed to be. After all, it's a sanctuary, a place to sit in silence and reflect or pray. "Tell them it's empty," she whispered to Jonah who was more than happy to dash back outside.

"Father Harris," Leanne called. No reply. Cautiously, she took a few steps down the aisle between the rows of pews. "Father Harris?" Still nothing.

"This place is well creepy!" Tommy announced as he stepped inside, his voice seeming even louder in the small space. His comment was met with a loud 'Shh!' from both girls.

"I don't think Harris is here," Leanne said. "There must be an office out back." The group made their way past the altar and found a closed door with Harris's name on it. Tommy reached for the handle, but Leanne stopped him. She knocked twice, straining to hear any movement coming from within.

Short Horror Stories Volume 3

Nothing.

Leanne nodded and Tommy turned the knob, relieved to find it unlocked. He led the way inside, scanning the dull room for anything worth taking. It only took a moment before Lizzy pointed to a stack of wine boxes in the corner. "Probably just some cheap stuff they get from a wholesaler, but better than nothing," she said, grabbing a box of six bottles. "This enough?"

"Plenty," Leanne muttered. As happy as she was to have some drinks with her friends, the thought of them clearing more than six bottles of red made her feel sick. "Plus, we're not going to want to carry more than that around."

"We should go then," Tommy suggested. "Silly to hang around."

"Quite right," a voice said in the doorway to the office, startling Lizzy to the point she almost dropped the box. Harris stood blocking their only way out, but he showed little sign of anger. "So, want to explain what you think you're doing?"

The four remained silent, eyes fixed on their shoes. After an awkward moment of silence, Lizzy took a few steps and placed the box of wine bottles where she had found it. "We'll go now. Sorry, Father," she said.

"It's fine," Harris said with a sigh. "Believe it or not, I was young once too. But you shouldn't be stealing. Or drinking, really."

"We know," Lizzy said. "We'll head back to the fete now. And we'll stay out of trouble."

P.J. Blakey-Novis

Father Harris stepped aside to let the group leave and they filed out, murmuring apologies. They'd made it halfway through the main area of the church when Harris heard Tommy say, "That was a close one. If he'd threatened to tell anyone, I might have had to offer your services Lizzy. But then he *is* a priest, so he'd much rather have a go on little Jonah here." Tommy laughed at his own joke, but the others just groaned, embarrassed by the volume at which Tommy spoke.

Harris felt something else entirely. Not embarrassment but anger. He was being ridiculed by this arrogant little prick and he'd had enough of turning the other cheek. Nothing good would come of Tommy, of that he was certain. Lizzy seemed like an airhead whose only aim in life was gaining followers online and clinging onto Tommy. The others seemed okay, saveable perhaps, but time would tell. After all the years spent here, guarding and protecting the church's secrets, Harris had finally had enough.

"Wait," he called after them. They were at the door by this point, Leanne at the back of the foursome.

"Yes?" she asked, turning to face the shadow of Father Harris at the far end of the church.

"That wasn't very welcoming of me," he explained. "I don't mean to be a killjoy. I know you shouldn't drink at your age, but we give wine to younger ones as part of

101

Short Horror Stories Volume 3

communion. Can you keep a secret?"

All four of the youngsters were huddled in the main doorway now, listening to Father Harris as he took small steps towards them.

"If you promise not to tell our parents we tried to take the wine, we can keep a secret," Lizzy promised.

"I was planning on having a couple of glasses of wine myself in a moment. You can join me, if you'd like. I know you'll end up drinking somewhere today, so I'd feel better if I was there to supervise."

"Sounds shit," Tommy mumbled but Lizzy elbowed him quickly.

"Free wine, and we don't have to search around for drinks elsewhere. Could be worse," Leanne whispered.

"Does it not seem creepy to you?" Tommy replied, as quietly as he could manage. "He's either going to bang on about God all afternoon, or he's after something else."

"I'm sure he will talk about making the right choices and God and Jesus and all that stuff. But I think he just wants to make sure we're safe," Leanne said.

"I'm in," Lizzy said, loudly enough for Harris to hear, before scurrying down the aisle to meet him.

Despite Leanne suggesting otherwise, Father Harris had handed Jonah a small glass of red wine. The boy didn't like the taste but peer pressure from Tommy, who Jonah certainly looked up to, meant that he

P.J. Blakey-Novis

managed to finish it and take another. Leanne set out to be restrained, taking her responsibility for her thirteen-year-old brother quite seriously, but after the third glass of red she began to go with the flow.

Tommy and Lizzy, of course, were necking as much cheap Claret as they could get a hold of in case Father Harris put an end to their bizarre little gathering. Harris, however, wasn't exactly pacing himself either. He was still raging within about Tommy's constant jibes and needed the drink in order to go through with the dangerous plan he had concocted. While Tommy feared Harris would throw them out at some point, the vicar was desperate to keep his guests there.

They discussed religion, naturally, along with their plans for the future and Harris gave a little history as to why he was there. Conversation began to dry up and Lizzy, becoming tired from all the red wine, eventually suggested leaving. Harris could wait no longer.

"There is more to my job than you'd expect," he said, glancing at each of them. Nobody seemed interested in hearing about preparing sermons or checking in on the elderly. "Did you know this church has a secret room downstairs?"

"Like a torture room for little boys?" Tommy asked, finding himself even more hilarious than when he was sober.

"No Tommy," Father Harris replied, forcing patience into his voice. "It's a collection of

103

Short Horror Stories Volume 3

artefacts the church keeps hidden. My role here is to guard them. To make sure nobody knows about them."

Lizzy started laughing. "Your job is to make sure nobody finds out about the secret room, so you tell us about it? You're not very good at your job, Father." Tommy started laughing along with her, but Leanne looked serious.

"What sort of artefacts?" she asked.

"All kinds of things. Evil things. Holy things. You'd be amazed."

"Bullshit," Tommy declared. "If there is even anything down there, it's probably old scrolls or coins or something."

"Why don't you come and take a look?" Harris suggested with a smirk.

The group watched as Father Harris dragged an old filing cabinet across the floor with a nasty squeak. It was just possible to make out the outline to a small door behind where the cabinet had been, but with no door handle. Harris pushed a part of the door gently and it opened a couple of inches. Grabbing the edge of the door, he pulled it the rest of the way and hit a switch.

Now he had everyone's attention and they gathered behind him, peering around to get a better look. The door didn't open into a room but a set of stairs going down. "What's down there really?" Lizzy asked.

"I've told you," Harris replied. "Old things. Come and see for yourself."

104

P.J. Blakey-Novis

Lizzy looked at Tommy, her eyes questioning. "Nah," Tommy said. "Sounds boring." The fear in his voice was unmistakable, however.

"If you're scared, I understand," Father Harris said. "A lot of evil is contained in that room."

The statement had the desired effect. "I ain't scared of nothing," Tommy lied. "Show us the old crap if you must, then we'll be heading off."

Father Harris led the group down into a small basement. Small, yet packed with glass-fronted cabinets and bookshelves. "Jeez," Leanne said, looking around. "It's like that room at the Warrens' house with all the haunted stuff."

"Have a look around," Harris offered. "I'm going to the loo. Anyone want another glass of wine while I'm up there?" Tommy gave a nod but nobody else answered, fascinated as they were by the displays.

Leanne heard Father Harris climbing the stairs back to his office, followed by what could have been the click of a lock. She pushed the thought from her mind as she looked about, running a hand across the spines of leather-bound titles on the bookshelf. There were books on all religions, some she had heard of, some far more obscure. There were books on the occult, on symbolism, witchcraft, and even books of spells.

Lizzy pointed at the bizarre items stored

Short Horror Stories Volume 3

behind glass, seemingly normal things which were alleged to be either cursed or possessed. A few creepy dolls, a pack of Tarot cards, a Ouija board with what looked a lot like blood smeared across it, a black fedora, and a vial of something deep red all filled the cabinet in the centre of the room.

Leanne discovered a filing cabinet in the corner, one which looked surprisingly normal amongst the oddities, and pulled open the first drawer. Inside were newspaper clippings, medical reports, eyewitness accounts, and photographs from exorcisms the church had performed. Disturbing images of people bent into unnatural shapes, some clearly deceased, spewed from the pages. The images frightened her, and she shoved them back with haste.

Reluctantly, Leanne opened the second drawer to find a similar collection, minus the photographs, but much older. Details of religious persecution filled the files – witches being burned at stakes, homosexuals being tortured until they begged for forgiveness, non-Catholics imprisoned and executed for daring to question the might of the Vatican. The files were shocking in their detail and Leanne struggled to stop reading until her thoughts were disrupted by the sound of breaking glass.

"Tommy!" Lizzy shrieked. "Harris is going to be so pissed at you!"

"Oops," Tommy slurred, a smile plastered on his face. "Think I've had enough wine now.

106

P.J. Blakey-Novis

But at least we can get to the stuff..."

Lizzy watched as Tommy reached a hand through the broken pane and into the centre cabinet. "What do you reckon this is?" he asked, holding up the vial of dark liquid. "Looks like blood."

"That's gross. Put it back," Lizzy ordered but Tommy slipped the vial into his pocket.

"The hat is cool, though," he remarked, pulling the fedora through the gap and placing it on his head at an angle. "Pretty gangster, yeah?"

"Makes you look old," Lizzy said. "And where is Father Harris? He's been ages."

"I'll go check. Come on Jonah," Leanne said, climbing the stairs. Only halfway up, it became evident that the door was closed. Attempting to suppress the feeling of panic welling up within her, Leanne reached for the door and gave it a push. No movement. She knocked, calling out for Harris. Silence. *He's locked us down here!* she thought, not daring to speak it aloud for fear of frightening Jonah.

She looked to her younger brother, only to see that he fully understood the situation. He turned, running down to find Tommy, certain that the older boy would be able to help. "Tommy!" Jonah yelled. "We're locked in. The door won't open!"

Lizzy paled, looking to Leanne for confirmation. Tommy just laughcd, ruffling Jonah's hair. "I'm sure the door just needs a bit more of a push. I'll see to it." Tommy took

Short Horror Stories Volume 3

to the stairs, his drunkenness now evident as he ran his hands along the walls for support. They could hear him kicking at the door, banging on it, shouting for the vicar to open up. All to no avail. Coming down the stairs proved even more challenging than going up them and Tommy slipped from almost the top. He rolled over, hitting the floor at the bottom with enough force to daze him.

"Oh my god, are you okay?" Lizzy squealed, rushing to his side. With Leanne's help, they managed to get Tommy into a sitting position. "You're bleeding!" Lizzy yelled, a look of disgust on her face.

Next to Tommy's pocket, a thick, almost black stain was spreading. Instinctively, he pushed a hand into the pocket and felt the sharp stab of broken glass. "Not my blood," he said, sounding relieved. "That little bottle was in my pocket, must have smashed when I hit the floor."

"That's nasty," Lizzy said, scrunching her nose. "That could be anybody's blood." Before Tommy could reply, the room was plunged into darkness.

Leanne awakened to find herself laying in damp grass, moonlight trying desperately to peek through the grey clouds. Her first thought was of Jonah, and she tried to sit herself up, discovering she was gagged, her wrists and ankles bound. Her second thought was to wonder how she got there, how much time had passed, and who had put her in this

108

P.J. Blakey-Novis

situation. It was hard to make out much in the darkness of the rural setting, but she soon became certain she was in the graveyard attached to the church.

Using her tongue to push the rag from her mouth, she called out, "Jonah!", more concerned for his safety than her own. A sound of movement came from behind her and she rolled herself over. There, bound as she was, Leanne spotted three others. The most obvious thought was that Jonah, Lizzy, and Tommy were in the same predicament. As her eyes adjusted to the darkness, she soon realised that this wasn't the case. Jonah was there, Lizzy was there, but that was not Tommy. That was an older man, a man wearing black with a white collar...a vicar.

"It's about time you woke up," came a voice she did not recognise. Moving her head to the side she saw a figure, a silhouette really. The voice did not match but she knew instantly that it was Tommy, still wearing that ridiculous hat.

"Tommy?" she croaked. "What's happening? You sound weird."

"I'm afraid Tommy can't come to the phone right now, he's a little busy."

"What are you talking about? Untie me!"

"I think Father Harris has some explaining to do," 'Tommy' said, stepping closer. "Now, I'll get the gags off you all, as long as you promise not to scream."

Leanne looked at the faces of her friends, each now a mask of terror. *Has Tommy*

Short Horror Stories Volume 3

snapped? Is this just a prank? He's gone too far this time. She watched as Tommy crouched in front of Lizzy and pulled the fabric from her mouth. As soon as she was able, the girl let out an ear-splitting scream. With inhuman speed, Tommy picked up a rock and thrust it into Lizzy's face. The first strike split her nose with a crunching sound and a whimper. By the tenth strike Lizzy didn't move at all.

"I said silence. Perhaps now you can see I meant it." Jonah began to sob and Leanne could feel tears welling up. Evidently this was no prank. "I can *hear* you crying. I said to be quiet..." Jonah managed to control his whimpering but the scent on the air suggested his bladder had released with fear.

"Better," Tommy said. "Now, Father Harris, would you like to tell our guests about your little collection? Surely you knew something like this was bound to happen when you locked them down there?" Tommy approached the vicar and yanked the gag away.

"I thought," began Harris, "that I'd lock them down there to frighten them. Tommy is a nasty little prick and I wanted to teach him a lesson. But no, I didn't think this would happen."

"Tommy certainly is wonderful, isn't he? He's still in here, somewhere. But not for long, I fear. What I'd like to know is why you even showed them the room? See, I think you're nothing but a fucking liar. Your job in

P.J. Blakey-Novis

this miserable world is protecting those items which makes me sure that you knew they wouldn't survive. But why? For a creature like me, it would just be sport. But for a man of the cloth to deliberately try to eliminate some poor, innocent children...well, I think you may be on the wrong side!"

"My motives are irrelevant now," Harris replied. "You know what I can do, the power I hold, my position in the church. It's time you went back."

Laughter filled the air as 'Tommy' wiped tears from his eyes. "What exactly do you think you can do? The only thing holding me in that musty room was the blood. *His* blood. Not quite so powerful when it's over some drunk kid's boxers, is it? Do you think your all-knowing god knew this would happen? That the blood of his only son would end up drying on some teenager's jeans in more than two-thousand years' time! What a hilarious fucking situation we find ourselves in."

"Just let us go," Leanne begged. "I don't know what's happening, but I just want to take my brother and go home."

'Tommy' smiled at Leanne, tipping his fedora. "How about I ignore the fact you spoke without permission and explain a little about what's happening? Would you like that?"

Leanne paused, trying to decide on the correct response. "I don't need to know anything. I'd rather just leave."

"I'm sure you fucking would! But you're

Short Horror Stories Volume 3

involved now." 'Tommy' turned to Harris. "This one seems pretty innocent, you know. Pretty shitty of you to put her and the young one through this."

Harris didn't reply, just sitting with his eyes fixed on the creature before him. In the darkness, Leanne could make out the Father's lips moving quickly, almost silently, as he began to recite something in a language she did not understand.

"We *are* innocent," Leanne pleaded. "Whatever your issue with Father Harris is, you don't need us."

"Oh, perhaps you misunderstand me," 'Tommy' replied. "I don't care in the slightest if you're innocent or not. You'll be mine tonight. As will your brother, and the rest of this shitty village. My vengeance will spread from here, surrounding the earth, claiming souls for Lucifer himself."

Leanne glanced at Harris, his eyes still fixed, mouth working on what could only be a prayer. Until that moment, Leanne believed prayers were useless. But then she also wouldn't have believed her friend could be possessed by a demon, leading him to smash his girlfriend's face in. Leanne decided her only chance would be to keep the monster talking and let Harris continue his recital.

"So, what are you?" Leanne asked.

"It's not particularly relevant but I suppose your kind would call me a demon."

"And you've been trapped here? Harris trapped you?"

112

P.J. Blakey-Novis

"That pathetic creature?" 'Tommy' asked with a chuckle. "Not him. He's just a caretaker. He keeps certain *items* secure. But as you can see, he's not very good at it."

"But someone trapped you. Someone brought you here," Leanne pressed.

"The hat..." Father Harris said suddenly. "The evil lives within that bastard hat. It's turned up all over the world, the wearer taking a different guise each time. The church managed to get it after that debacle in London at the Castle Heights tower block."

"That's right Harris, tell her everything. That way I'll have even less reason to let her go."

"As if you would anyway," Harris replied, and Leanne's heart sank at the words. She took a look towards Jonah who remained still on the ground. He was staring ahead as he lay on his side, his chest moving with each breath, but he gave no other signs of life. *Is he in shock?* Leanne wondered.

"What now then?" Leanne asked, trying to distract the creature in the hope that Harris could find a way to end this.

"Well, as I said," 'Tommy' began, "I'm going to take your soul. And Jonah's. I don't want Harris's though. Filthy fucking thing, I'm sure. Fear helps the process, and it seems little Jonah may be as frightened as it's possible to be, so he'll be first."

"No!" screamed Leanne, yanking hard at her binds. "Leave him alone!" With all her might, Leanne tried to shuffle herself along

Short Horror Stories Volume 3

the ground towards her brother. Hips bruised and shoulders sore, she moved painfully slowly as 'Tommy' stood over her in hysterics.

"Would you find it easier if I removed your restraints?" he offered with a smirk. He waved a hand theatrically and Leanne felt her wrists and ankles release. She eyed the monster suspiciously as she pulled herself onto her knees.

"And Jonah's?" she asked.

"Sure, why not? I'm in a good mood." The creature waved a hand once more, this time in the opposite direction, and Leanne heard a sickening crunch followed by a scream. Jonah rolled onto his back, four jets of blood spraying from the end of each limb. "Oops," Tommy said. "My bad. Did the waving thingy the wrong way. Righty tighty, lefty loosey. Sorry about that."

Leanne lunged for what used to be Tommy, her rage animalistic. All she could think of was to pull him to the ground and pummel him with a rock. She came within a few inches of his legs before his shoe connected with her jaw, landing with such force she was thrown halfway across the cemetery.

Bloody, battered and bruised, Leanne tried to stand, making it as far as getting to her knees. She knew Jonah was almost certainly dead and she felt nothing but contempt for Father Harris for placing them in this situation. She wanted to run, to take advantage of the distance between herself and the demon. But what of Jonah? What if

P.J. Blakey-Novis

he could still be saved?

'Tommy' seemed busy with Harris, gloating about his plans for world domination, so Leanne began a painful crawl towards her brother. She had no idea what powers this monster possessed but did her best to creep along, knowing she couldn't live with herself if she abandoned the boy. She came within six feet of Jonah before she could make out anything more than a shadow on the ground. He was completely still and the faint light of the moon was just enough for Leanne to see his eyes were open. Open, yet glazed over. There was no gentle rise and fall of his chest.

Holding in a wail of sorrow, Leanne began crawling backwards, trying to put enough space between herself and the monster before scrambling to her feet and running. The darkness was thick, and she did her best to block out the creature's monologue as he lectured Harris on how powerful a demon he really was. A cracking sound made Leanne's heart skip as she realised she had knelt on a twig. She chanced a glance at the monster, but he was still preoccupied with the vicar.

Deciding that was her moment, she slowly rose to her feet. She took careful steps towards the edge of the churchyard under the cloak of darkness. *Is it too dark for him to see me?* she wondered. The question soon became redundant as the sky was lit up with fireworks. A series of multi-coloured bursts illuminated the frightened girl and she froze as 'Tommy' turned his head towards her.

Short Horror Stories Volume 3

Their eyes met and she ran.

The demon moved his hands about in the air for a moment and Leanne felt her feet leave the ground. Her legs continued to work as though she were running, even as she was pulled back into the cemetery. She screamed, as loudly as she could, but even Harris struggled to hear her over the fireworks.

"Time's up," the creature said, and as the final explosion of light lit up the sky, Leanne's spine cracked, folding her in half as she floated above the ancient graves. A few more horrific snaps and Leanne's arms and legs wrapped themselves around her broken body. "Ta, da," 'Tommy' said, letting the girl's body drop to the ground. "Just us now..." Harris hadn't stopped reciting the Latin prayers, despite them seeming to be next to useless. The demon showed no sign of caring what the vicar was mumbling. "Well, that was dramatic..." it said, glancing down at what was left of Leanne.

"I'm getting a bit bored now," 'Tommy' said with a sigh. "You'd probably have more luck with those prayers if you worked on your Latin. Pronunciation is everything, you know."

Seemingly undeterred, Harris kept up his mumbling, refusing to look away or react to anything the demon said.

"ENOUGH!" the creature roared with sufficient force that Harris paused for a moment. His bravado was slipping and something akin to fear finally showed on his

116

P.J. Blakey-Novis

face. "I've toyed with you long enough, *Father.*"

"So kill me already," Harris said. "I'm ready to take my place in Paradise."

'Tommy' howled with genuine laughter. "Paradise?" he spat. "You really think that's where you'll go? After what you did? I don't think a priest who deliberately puts innocent children in harm's way, who releases a fucking demon, is going *up*. Lucifer can have your soul if he wants it; it's certainly not something I'd want to consume."

"Demons lie," Harris stated casually. "Where my soul ends up is not your decision anyway. So make your move – I'm ready."

'Tommy' launched himself at the vicar, raising Harris's head and slamming it against a broken headstone, once, twice, three times. The man was out cold but still breathing and the monster stood over him deep in thought. The world was his for the taking but he still needed to be careful.

Shortly before ten, a flash of lightning signified the beginning of a storm. The heavy clap of thunder followed only seconds after, and the ground was saturated with rain within minutes. The downpour, wherever it came from, was heavier than anyone had experienced for years.

Just in time, Harris thought, surveying the cemetery. Four fresh graves had been dug for four poor teenagers. He knew their disappearance would take some explaining

Short Horror Stories Volume 3

but the kids had done nothing but complain about the boring village. Why would anyone be *that* surprised if they'd run off together on some teenage adventure? *Perhaps another glass of wine?* he mused.

Stepping inside the church, Harris grabbed a small towel from the bathroom and dried his face. He slipped his shoes off, poured himself a large glass of communion wine, and got comfortable in the office chair. He caught a glimpse of his reflection in the glass frame of a print on the wall. *The hat suits me,* he thought with a smirk.

P.J. Blakey-Novis

Doomsday

Satan sat at his ornate desk of human bones and glanced at the clock. *Almost time,* he mused. He had ordered the clock to run in sync with what humans called the Doomsday Clock, a metaphorical prediction as to when the world would end. Satan had marvelled at how quickly the hands had moved over the last century, motivated by global warming, deforestation, and man's lust for nuclear war. This past Earth-year or two brought a new virus, and the time to strike was almost here.

"Stupid humans," he muttered. "They've done this to themselves." He allowed himself a grin, more than happy to unleash Hell and finish humanity for good. Of course, he could have done this any time he chose to, but watching them destroy themselves was just as satisfying. The Earth was beyond the point of no return, now it would just be a free-for-all to claim souls. He just needed to strike before God decided he'd finally make his second coming.

"I just don't see the point anymore," Leo admitted. "Everything has gone to shit. Humanity is just as much a virus as Covid."

"So what do you suggest?" his wife asked. "What can we do about any of it?"

"Nothing. The world's fucked, there's no going back from that. I just want to know

Short Horror Stories Volume 3

what happens next, after we die."

"You're forty, Leo. You aren't going to die any time soon." Mary pushed her chair back from the breakfast bar and stood. "You can be quite dramatic, you know," she said with a smile.

"It is time!" Satan bellowed, his voice reverberating around the enormous cavern. The group he addressed were a frightening spectacle; demons of all shapes and sizes cheered and screamed, many of whom had been waiting for this day for centuries.

"Today, now, we strike. We hit humanity at its weakest, and we take their souls. But listen to me..." He paused, ensuring his minions were paying attention. "...willing souls are what we want. Torture them all you like, just make sure they offer themselves unto me."

With a demonic battle-cry, Satan and all who gathered before him vanished from Hell.

"Sorry," Leo mumbled. "I just feel lost, I suppose. Everything is so depressing. Nothing is fun anymore." Mary looked hurt. "Shit, I didn't mean it like that. You know what I mean."

"Do I?" she asked with a sigh. "Yeah, the world seems pretty shitty right now. The news is beyond upsetting, lockdown is a real struggle, but we have each other. We're lucky compared to so many others. Everything will get better, I..." Mary's attempt at reassurance

P.J. Blakey-Novis

was cut short by a scream from the street. Then another. And more, until it sounded as though the whole neighbourhood was joining in.

Leo rushed to the window, pulling the net curtain to one side for a better view. "Holy fuck!" He turned to his wife. "Everything will get better?" he asked, eyes wide with panic.

Mary joined him and let out a shriek of her own at the sight of people being terrorised in the street. Creatures, ugly beyond description, chased them, whipped and clawed at them. "What are they?" Mary whispered. Leo just stared, mouth open. "Leo!" she said, grabbing at his arm. "We need to go."

Leo snapped out of his trance and nodded, eyes darting around the room for his car keys. He grabbed them from a side table and slipped on his shoes and jacket. "Quietly," he ordered, approaching the front door. Mary nodded as she slipped into her hoody.

The door opened silently, much to the couple's relief. Whatever those monsters were, they seemed too busy rounding people up to notice as Leo unlocked the car. Waiting until Mary was in and buckled, Leo started the engine, ready to make a fast escape. The sound of the car was muffled by the surrounding screams but still did no go unnoticed. Two hideous beings watched them leave, their gazes fixed firmly on Mary.

As Leo gunned the car to the next crossing, he risked a glance in his rear-view mirror.

Short Horror Stories Volume 3

"What the fuck?" he muttered, his eyes now transfixed on the sight behind him. A huge figure had appeared within the chaos, blood-red skin, hooves for feet, horns sharp enough to gut a man. "Is that...?"

Leo managed to return his eyes to the road and took a left turn, pushing the car to speeds he never thought it could manage. "Did you see that?" he asked, turning quickly to Mary.

"You mean Satan?" she asked, no hint of shock or surprise in her voice. Leo didn't answer. "I did see him, yes. As I have seen him many times before. He is our Lord and Master, Leo. He has come to save us from this pitiful existence."

Leo hit the brakes, bringing the car to a screeching halt. He checked the mirror to ensure nothing had followed them, before cautiously looking at his wife. "Sorry?" was all he could manage.

"You were right, Leo. Humanity has run its course. The Day of Reckoning is upon us. You wanted to know what came next, after this life. Today you get to decide which way you will go. Up..." Mary glanced at the roof of the car for emphasis, "or DOWN!" This last word came from Mary's throat but sounded nothing like her. Not feminine, not even human. Leo fumbled for the handle and swung the door open, getting tangled in his seatbelt.

"What's happening?" he screamed, still trying to unclip himself.

122

P.J. Blakey-Novis

"Give me your fucking soul!" 'Mary' bellowed, fingers scratching at his face. Finally, Leo found the release button and fell backwards into the road. In an instant, she was on him. Leo watched in terror as her once beautiful face began to contort. Her eyes bugged, teeth began to blacken before him. Ears changed shape, taking on a pointed appearance.

"Mary!" Leo yelled.

"I'm sorry, Mary is unavailable at the moment. If you want to see her, you know what to do," the demon sneered.

A thought process began in Leo's mind, seemingly coming from nowhere. As he tried to fathom the situation he found himself in, something didn't add up.

"You want my soul?" The words felt unnatural, the reality of his situation not hitting home yet.

"Yessss," hissed the creature on top of him.

"But you need me to offer it up?"

"We can make you do that," it said, jabbing a nail into Leo's left eye.

Leo screamed through the pain, took a breath, and then said, "But Mary didn't offer you hers." Leo knew he couldn't be entirely sure, but at the same time doubted that his wife would do anything quite so stupid, even if she had been told to. He saw something in the eyes which met his, a slight shift. As though the monster had been caught out.

With an almighty screech, Mary's body

Short Horror Stories Volume 3

shuddered before slumping to the ground beside Leo. "Mary?" he asked, tentatively touching her shoulder. Slowly, her eyes opened. They looked different – more her own.

"Leo?" she said, her confusion evident. "What happened? I remember getting into the car then everything went blank."

"I don't know," Leo lied, seeing no benefit to telling his wife she had been possessed by a demonic entity, even for a short while.

"What happened to your eye?" Mary asked, raising a hand to her husband's face.

"Don't worry about it. I caught it getting out of the car." Another lie and Leo was sure this was the most dishonest he had ever been with Mary. "We need to get out of here."

"I want them all!" Satan bellowed from one of the lawns on what was a previously quiet street. He surveyed the melee before him, as his multitudes of nightmarish creatures tortured the humans they found. A winged monstrosity almost eight feet tall had two women skewered on the ends of his talons, demanding their souls as they slowly bled out. A creature that appeared no more physical than a shadow screeched as it literally flew *through* people, silencing their screams as it did so. Minor demons, imps, dwarves, and other lower beings terrorized the children of the neighbourhood, chasing them with scalding metal and razor-sharp weapons. Hell on Earth had begun in the

P.J. Blakey-Novis

sleepy town and would spread across the globe.

"Where do we go?" Mary asked, her face a mix of confusion and terror. "Where could possibly be safe? The police?"

Leo grunted a short laugh. "I don't think the police will be much use against the forces of Hell. And I have no doubt that is what we are running from. Mary," he said, taking his eyes from the road to look her in the eye, "this could be the Day of Reckoning. There is only one place that *might* be safe. Church."

Neither Mary nor Leo had set foot inside a church since a funeral they attended for a friend several years ago. Until this day, neither had anything even resembling a faith. A curiosity about an afterlife, perhaps, but not a faith in anything real or good. Leo did notice something unexpected, however. Perhaps not as unexpected as Satan and a horde of demons showing up on their street and claiming their neighbours' souls, but unexpected, nonetheless. Leo wanted to live. For more than a year he had felt less than enthusiastic about life, unable to make any changes to his situation, bored beyond belief. Now, more than ever before, he had a purpose – to stay alive, to save his wife, maybe even to save the world. His thoughts quickly moved to the fantastical as he daydreamed of himself as the slayer of demons, but Mary soon put an end to the fantasies.

Short Horror Stories Volume 3

"Church!" she shouted, causing Leo to focus again on where he was driving and he pulled onto the gravel parking area beside the small, 15th century structure.

Leo looked out the car windows in all directions, checking they had not been followed this far, before opening his door cautiously. Once Mary had safely exited, he pressed the button to lock the vehicle and took her hand, leading her to the solid wooden door of the church and pushing it open.

The place smelled of wood polish and dust. The darkness within barely pierced by streams of light through grimy stained-glass windows. "Hello?" Leo called, confident that someone should be in the building. The pair took a few steps along the aisle between pews, each footstep echoing against ancient stone. "Hello?"

Mary let out a yelp as something moved ahead of them. Something black, only a few feet in height. The lack of light bathed everything in shadow and the couple were about to run when the shape rose.

"Yes?" it said, and Leo released the breath he had been subconsciously holding.

"Jesus," Leo muttered, allowing a chuckle to escape on seeing the priest, all dressed in black, move from a kneeling position to standing.

"Not quite," the priest replied. "But if you're looking for Him, you're in the right place."

"Sorry," Leo said, embarrassed by his

P.J. Blakey-Novis

blasphemy. "We need your help, though."

"Because the Day of Reckoning is upon us and you fear for your immortal souls?"

Leo looked at Mary, surprised this priest knew so much already. "Yes, something like that," he admitted.

"Well then, let's see what we can do about the situation. Come." The priest pointed to a pew in the front row and took a seat beside them. "There have been various predictions about when this day would arrive, from the Mayans to interpretations of the Bible, among other religious books, to the scientists responsible for the Doomsday Clock. It seems that the scientists came closest to getting it right but no surprise there. However, that's fairly irrelevant now. What matters is how we proceed."

"I don't know much about this stuff," Mary explained. "But is this not the day that Jesus is supposed to come back?"

The priest looked thoughtful. "Supposed to, yes. And perhaps He will. Or maybe it's just another test, to see who gives in to Satan. Perhaps our Lord and Saviour is content with whatever souls are left."

"Seems a bit harsh," Leo said, immediately regretting it.

"In what way?" the priest asked, no judgment in his voice.

"Well," Leo began, selecting his words carefully. "Does God only want souls from whoever is strong enough to bear the torture of demons? Is He unwilling to come to

Short Horror Stories Volume 3

humanity's aid, in one big showdown with the Devil? I'm sure there would be a lot of new believers if they saw God and Devil fighting things out."

The priest let out a sigh. "I think the Bible stories about this day are, unfortunately, fantastical ideas of what *could* happen, rather than what *will*. More Hollywood than reality. I'm afraid the only way to ascend will be to stay strong throughout whatever ordeal awaits us."

"Couldn't we offer our souls to God and then die before these monstrosities find us?" Mary suggested, tears welling in her eyes.

"And how do you plan to die, my dear?" the priest asked. "We cannot kill one another, nor ourselves, for both would send us straight to Satan's pit. The chances of us having a fatal accident before we face off against these nightmares is slim at best."

"Then we fight?" Leo asked, terrified but pumped with adrenalin.

"We fight," the priest replied with a nod and a grin.

The denizens of Hell had spread out in all directions from the street Mary and Leo had called home, so it took more than an hour for the sounds of screaming and the smell of charred flesh to reach the small church. Enough time for the motley trio to stand guard at the open door, armed with blessed and makeshift weapons.

"Don't forget to pray," the priest reminded

P.J. Blakey-Novis

Leo. "We've been over the words, just keep on repeating them. Loudly. That should keep the smaller ones at bay."

"It's not the smaller ones I'm worried about," Mary said, a crucifix in one hand and a large, silver goblet in the other.

"Now, there is no way we can take them all out. We're grossly outnumbered and they are pure evil from the bowels of Hell. We have enough holy water to defend ourselves for a while, but the big guy needs to be our priority."

"Satan?" Leo said, unable to hide the shock on his face. "You want us, *us,* to do what exactly? To kill the Devil?"

"Of course not," the priest chuckled. "But we can send that fucker back to Hell."

The expletive came as a shock and sent the trio into fits of laughter. "Amen to that, Father," Mary managed. The confidence they had briefly felt all but disappeared at the sight of winged beasts approaching.

"Can they come in?" Leo asked. "I mean, physically. What with it being holy ground or whatever."

"I don't fancy finding out," the priest said, "and we don't have anything to take down the flying ones."

Leathery wings flapped loudly as the demons snatched adults and children from the streets, tossing them to one another. A few times they missed, bodies hitting the street with a blood-soaked splat.

"Should we be doing anything?" Mary

129

Short Horror Stories Volume 3

whispered. "Some of them are just children." She was barely holding back tears, but her face was hard, angry and determined.

"We wait," the priest ordered. "It's the big guy we want."

They didn't have to wait long. The ground shook before they could even see the oncoming swarm. A shrill screeching filled the air as hundreds of imps and goblins moved as one; a stampede of pure evil, heading directly for the church.

"It's time," Leo said, holding out the bucket of holy water, two crucifixes in the sides of his jeans like a demon-slaughtering gunslinger. The wave of dark power kept coming. There were too many of them, Leo realised. There was no way they would even make a dent in the onslaught. Then something happened that none of them expected. Not more than twenty feet from the entrance to the church, the swarm split in two. Half spread to the right side of the church, the other half to the left, before re-joining on the road behind and continuing in the direction they had been headed. It was as though they could not step on hallowed ground.

"They can't come in," Mary gasped, suddenly feeling a lot more confident as she watched thousands of hellish creatures dart past. The rumbling of the ground changed noticeably, from the dull shake of the swarm of beasts, to something more akin to giant footsteps.

P.J. Blakey-Novis

"He's coming," the priest said.

Satan spied the small church, sensed the three souls available for the picking. His minions could deal with the general population. He wanted the prized targets, the churches, the harder to claim souls. He wanted priests, vicars, reverends, Sunday school teachers, organists. And when he'd claimed them all, he'd take the Pope.

Standing at the entrance to the building, holding an assortment of makeshift weapons, stood three humans. Satan sniffed the air, focusing. One stank deliciously of religious fervour and Satan felt a quickening of his black heart. One, the woman, smelled tainted, as though she had already been to the dark side. The man only gave off hints of fear. The couple would die first, then the bastard priest. Satan stepped towards the church, ignoring the calamity surrounding him as demons feasted and humans bled.

"You cannot enter this holy place, Lucifer!" screamed the priest, raising a worn, leather Bible.

"Oh?" Satan replied, a bemused look on his face. "Shall I just go then?" With this, he erupted into laughter.

"Now," whispered the priest and Leo and Mary began to shout the prayers they had been taught. There was a glimmer of hope as Satan's laugh ceased and he took a step back. The priest joined with the praying and

Short Horror Stories Volume 3

Satan couldn't hold his composure any longer, falling into another fit of laughter.

"You'd have more luck if you worked on the pronunciation a little," he explained. "But enough of this fooling around. Anyone want to offer me their soul willingly?"

Leo struck, throwing the holy water and catching Satan's lower leg. There was a hiss as it made contact, a smell of burning sulphur, and a roar loud enough to shatter the church's windows.

"Well, that seems to sting, you big red fuck," Leo shouted. The anger on the Devil's face soon sent Leo and the others retreating into the church.

The door came down with a crash, brushed aside by the hulking form of Satan. Crucifixes were held out, having no effect. Crucifixes were then thrown, either bouncing feebly off the thick red hide or missing altogether.

Mary, tears streaming, backed her way to the pulpit first. "If I give you my soul, will you spare the others?" Everyone froze in place.

Leo turned to his wife. "What are you doing?" he mouthed.

She ignored her husband and fixed the Devil with a glare. "Well?"

"Fine," Satan said.

"Stay away from her," Leo yelled, but dared not take a step towards the enemy.

"You offer your soul willingly?" Satan asked Mary, his voice calm and measured.

"I do," she replied, looking to her husband

P.J. Blakey-Novis

as tears fell. "I love you, Leo."

There was a whooshing sound, followed by the husk of Mary's earthly form dropping to the marble floor. The Devil let out a satisfied sigh as Leo dropped to his knees, overcome with grief.

"Now, where was I?" Satan mused. "Oh yes, taking souls..."

"What are you doing?" Leo yelled. "You promised!"

"I did no such thing!" the Devil replied. "And anyway, everyone knows I'm a liar, that's like my main thing. Stupid humans, no wonder you've managed to bring this all on. Can't even look after one planet properly. You can be with her, you know. Give me your soul and I'll reunite you both."

"No chance," Leo screamed, getting to his feet. "You just said you're a liar. I'm sending you back to Hell." He threw himself at Satan, arms swinging, set to kill. If his opponent had been human, Leo would have beaten the man to death. As it happened, Satan struck first, a punch with enough force to launch Leo to the back of the church and smash his head against the cold stone wall. Satan sighed again before rolling his shoulders and stretching his arms as though he were a boxer preparing for the next round.

"He's dead?" the priest asked.

"Almost," Satan replied. "Skull is all cracked, bleeding on the brain. Won't take long now."

"And I'm next?"

Short Horror Stories Volume 3

"Naturally. I'd prefer to take you willingly, though. Someone with your strength could be useful to my cause."

"My allegiances lie elsewhere," the priest said with quiet confidence.

"I understand. It's admirable, honestly. But your God isn't here to help you. I am, though. I can give you a future by my side. Do you really think you'll get into heaven anyway? I know the things you've done."

"Which is what exactly?" the priest countered. "A few scuffles, a bit of porn, a couple of years misspent in my youth. All repented, all forgiven."

"Hmm," Satan murmured. "So long as you're sure."

There was a creeping doubt niggling at the back of the priest's mind, but he ushered it away. His God loved him, he was certain of it. This was the final test. He knew he would die now, that it would be painful, but that Paradise waited for him.

"Last chance. Do you offer your soul willingly?" the Devil hissed.

"My soul belongs to God the Father, the Son, and the Holy Spirit," the priest said. Within a second, Satan was on him. One scorching red hand around his throat, the other yanking the priest's right arm free of its socket. The grip against his windpipe kept the scream buried and the priest closed his eyes. It would soon be over.

Satan threw the man a few feet into the air, catching him again by his throat but with

P.J. Blakey-Novis

the other hand. The priest's left arm was now flung across the pews, a bloody trail splashing on polished wood. The Devil eased his grip a little and raised his eyebrows, allowing the man to speak. Nothing.

"Too bad," Satan said with a shrug, before twisting the priest's head clean off his shoulders. The body dropped to the floor as Satan held the head in the air. "When I've devoured this world, heaven is next. I'll see you soon."

Short Horror Stories Volume 3

The Long Con

God exists! The thought hit Miranda, realisation bringing with it a renewed sense of terror. *All powerful. Ever loving. Eternally silent.* Something was wrong with the balance of things, something vastly... opposite, to what she had been taught.

Miranda grew up in the church, Sunday school every week, church camps with the youth groups. She reached seventeen and started to have doubts, the kind which plague all believers at some point in their lives. At an age when boys, drinking, and generally having fun were on her mind, Miranda felt being a 'good' Christian was too much of a gamble to miss out on the kind of teenage adventures which shape our lives.

Now, at twenty-seven and having not set foot inside a church for almost ten years, Miranda had reached the most unsettling of conclusions. Not only had she been wrong to dismiss His existence, He wasn't the 'good guy'. Suddenly it felt as though everything she knew had changed.

While this revelation was sudden, if Miranda considered the blur of the past few weeks more carefully, she'd see that a number of events had led her to this point. Watching the evening news does little to inspire belief in an all-loving God but ... what if He truly exists and yet chooses to do nothing about the horrors on Earth? Surely, that makes Him the enemy. And her son, Charlie, could confirm this.

From a mind that was nothing if not logical, Miranda extrapolated these thoughts. *An all-powerful God exists yet allows suffering. Therefore, He is the bad guy. If He exists, so does the Devil, the opposite of God, and, ergo, the Devil is the good one.*

There were flaws in her logic, she was aware of this, but overall she felt it was solid. *If you look at what the supposed Devil has given us... sex, drugs, and rock 'n' roll... they seem like the good things in life. And if you follow the theory that Hell is simply an absence of Heaven when we die, there is no great risk in the long-term.* These ideas were then compounded by the fact God and his followers 'bully' people into believing in Him – worship me or burn for eternity doesn't sound like the mantra of a loving creator. *The Devil worshippers have it right!*

In the last month, Miranda had lost the only two people who mattered to her – her son, Charlie, and her long-term boyfriend, Daniel. The first to drowning, the latter to such intense grief that he had walked away. *Too many reminders here,* he had said, suitcase in hand. Miranda understood, would have happily run away *with* Daniel, but *she* was the biggest reminder and how does one run away from oneself?

These tragedies alone would have

Short Horror Stories Volume 3

destroyed Miranda's faith if any had remained. Now, in an ironic twist, they compounded the existence of supreme beings. Because Charlie came back.

It had been almost four weeks since Charlie fell into that damned pond, and now here he stood, still fully clothed and dripping on the living room rug. That once roguish face now bloated with death, yet his eyes conveyed a happiness at seeing his mother again. The month had been a whirlwind of shock, despair, and disbelief, interspersed with funeral plans, fights with Daniel... and so much guilt. *Why weren't you watching him? Had you been drinking? He was only five, for fuck's sake Miranda!* Now a weight lifted, a recognition that there was more to life, and Miranda felt renewed.

"Charlie?" she asked, no doubt that he was real, no fear of *what* stood before her. "Charlie, come to Mummy." The boy took a few steps forward, his eyes transfixed on his mother. He looked confused more than anything, as though he had awoken from an all-too-vivid dream.

"Mummy, I think I fell asleep in the bath." It seemed a logical analysis for a five-year-old. "I had a bad dream."

As he approached, Miranda reached out her hands, half-expecting them to pass through him but he was solid. Touchable. *Real.* "You're soaked and freezing, Charlie. Let's get you under a hot shower and into

P.J. Blakey-Novis

some clean clothes." Miranda breathed a sigh of relief she had ignored Daniel's demands to empty Charlie's room.

"What did you dream?" she asked, peeling away the wet clothes. "Do you want to tell me about it?"

Charlie shook his head. "I don't know. It was scary. I was in a bad place. Everyone looked funny, like they were wearing girly dresses and they were all kneeling on the ground. I tried to copy but I must have done it wrong. A man in a black dress started hitting me."

Miranda reached a hand under the water to check the temperature before placing Charlie beneath the stream. His entire, bloated body was a sickly blue-grey hue. He flinched at the touch of water, as though it was bringing back the trauma from the pond, but he remained in place and allowed his mother to wash him gently with a sponge. Miranda ignored the smell of decay emanating from him, lathering her child in soap, and lovingly cleaning his hair as she pondered his words.

Dresses? Nuns and priests? Kneeling in prayer? Heaven, presumably, where all children should go. 'I was in a bad place.' Those words haunted her, compounding her ideas about God and the Devil. But how was Charlie back?

"Can I get dry now?" Charlie asked, snapping Miranda out of her thoughts. The boy looked cleaner, certainly, but no more

Short Horror Stories Volume 3

alive. She lifted him onto the bathmat and began drying him with a towel, but he cried out.

"Does that hurt?" she asked, puzzled. He nodded, looking down and watching a yellowy substance dribble down his legs. Miranda pulled the towel away and retched at both the sight and the smell. The towel had taken a layer of the boy's rotten flesh from his torso, black blood and flakes of dead skin visible. "I'm so sorry, I'll get a bandage."

As gently as she could manage, Miranda checked the child for open wounds, treated them, and dressed the boy in the softest pyjamas he owned. "Want to watch cartoons? Are you hungry?"

"Not hungry," he replied, making his way to the sofa and reaching for the television remote. Miranda helped find something for Charlie to watch, all the time wondering if he would need to even eat again. Or sleep. Or use the bathroom. *Would he age or be forever five?*

Satisfied that the boy was occupied, Miranda took a seat on the armchair opposite, notepad in hand. She had always been a 'pen and paper' type of person, forever making lists and organising what she called her 'overstocked mind' with notes and thoughts written out clearly.

Charlie's return was all she could have wished for but there were so many questions. She wrote out as many as she could think of, determined to find answers to each and every

P.J. Blakey-Novis

one. The major issue that she felt could cause serious problems was keeping him hidden. She lived in a small town, everyone had heard about the tragedy, so Miranda couldn't very well take Charlie to the shops with her. Neither did she want to leave him home alone. *Could he die again?* She added the question to her list. Her employer had given her 'indefinite compassionate leave', but she'd have to return one day.

However, the question that burned most vigorously wasn't about the future with Charlie, exactly. It was about *everyone's* future, after death. And what, or who, had actually returned Charlie to her.

"Charlie?" she began, his face covered in a smile as he watched the cartoons, oblivious to the splitting at the corners of his mouth. No response. "Charlie?" she tried again, and he looked in her direction expectantly.

"That dream you had," she began, dreading having to tell him he was dead. That was most certainly a conversation for another time. "Do you remember how you got away from the bad place?"

"Someone took me," he said with shrug.

"I don't understand," Miranda admitted.

"He looked like a monster. I was scared but then I wasn't. He took us all."

"All? He took everyone?"

"Just the kids. Like me. Said I was in the wrong place. A bad place. Then I woke up." Charlie started laughing at the brightly coloured antics on the television and Miranda

Short Horror Stories Volume 3

watched a lump of grey flesh fall from his cheek. Charlie didn't seem to notice.

Reaching for her phone, Miranda was online in a moment. Searching. *Child returns from the dead.* Skipping the Bible stories about Lazarus and near-death experiences, she found multiple accounts. *Similar* accounts but not the same. 'Dead Child Returns Home the Following Day'. 'Family's Shock as Dead Baby Comes Back to Life Hours Later'. And then a hundred or so ghost stories, parents so torn with grief they imagined seeing the mangled corpses of children lost to car accidents, school shootings, cancer. Nothing concrete.

Resigned to the fact she would discover nothing more about the afterlife from her child, Miranda was stuck. Who would know the answers to her questions? Who could possibly *truly* know? *A priest would just give me the bullshit narrative I was brought up with. What's the opposite of a priest? A Satanist? What did they even believe really?* Logic gave her some hope in the confusion, a ray of light through clouds of mystery. *People are inherently good,* she thought. *Despite all the horrors in the world, most people just want good things to happen. If people choose to worship the Devil, they must accept the existence of God, yet opt not to pray to Him. Do they know something most don't?* Miranda decided that would be the place to start.

She wasn't surprised to find no Satanic cults or devil-worshipping covens in her

P.J. Blakey-Novis

small town, but she'd also had no intention of meeting with anyone in person and leaving Charlie at home (or taking him outside, for that matter). But there were a multitude of online forums dedicated to all things occult and she quickly found herself falling down that particular rabbit hole.

The hours passed, Charlie in front of the television and smiling like he was just discovering his favourite shows for the first time, Miranda ruling out chat rooms full of goth teens and the ones calling for destruction and anarchy. What she was searching for was something more... mature? Relatable? Less terrifying?

It wasn't until night came fully, with Charlie still staring wide-eyed at the television, that Miranda found something with potential. She'd been feeling tired, about to give up on her search for the night but saw that Charlie wouldn't be sleeping. Probably ever again. *How will I keep him safe? I can't stay awake forever!*

Brewing more coffee, Miranda moved to the hard chairs at the dining room table, hoping the slight discomfort would keep her awake longer. There was a website she had found called The Long Con. On the homepage it featured the quote, *The greatest trick the Devil ever pulled was convincing the world he didn't exist.* She was sure it was from the Bible, but it made her think of the movie *The Usual Suspects* first. The quote was followed by a

143

Short Horror Stories Volume 3

'False Information' stamp, like you'd see on social media when someone has been ranting about the Earth being flat or vaccines causing autism.

The website looked amateur from the use of Comic Sans and enthusiastic exclamation points, but the message made sense. Under the original quote, it read *The greatest trick God ever pulled was convincing the world He was the good guy.* Everything she had been thinking was summed up in that sentence. Thousands of years of religion, mythos, fairy tales, and dogma all just a hoax. Miranda found the contact form and sent a message.

I need to know more. My son died last month. Now he's here, dead but not dead. He went somewhere after he died, somewhere he called 'bad', but I don't think it was Hell. I think he went to whatever passes for Heaven and the Devil rescued him. I need your help.

Returning to the armchair, Miranda fell into an uncomfortable sleep.

Waking as the early hints of sunlight crept through a gap in the curtains, Miranda's first observation was that Charlie hadn't moved. He still sat exactly as he had when she had fallen asleep, grinning at cartoon dragons, mesmerised. Then she noticed he looked worse, if it's possible to look worse than dead. His hands rested on his knees as he leaned forward, absorbed by the screen before him, but the backs of his hands had noticeable holes in them. *They weren't like that*

144

P.J. Blakey-Novis

yesterday.

Tentatively, she moved to sit beside her child and realised something which gave her pause. She was afraid of him, of his being there, of his lack of movement, of the clumps of bloated, dead flesh falling from him. "Charlie?" she said, unable to bring herself to touch him. "How are you feeling? Are you hungry?" He looked up at her, his grin punctuated with rotten teeth.

"I'm okay," he said cheerily as a piece of his neck flaked onto the sofa. "Not hungry."

"Well, what would you like to do today?" Miranda asked, trying to think of something that didn't involve leaving the house. "We could do some painting... or bake some cakes?"

"Not hungry," Charlie reminded her. "I'm watching TV." Then he turned back to the screen, staring into the blur of colour.

Miranda made coffee and checked her phone, a nervous flutter coming over her when she saw an email from *The Long Con.com.* Glancing up to check Charlie hadn't moved, she opened the email as she took a seat.

Fascinating! The message began, the excitement of the sender doing nothing to quell Miranda's unease. *From what you have said, it sounds like the first real evidence of our theory. Could we meet? May I speak with the boy?*

Miranda hesitated. Then looked at her sweet five-year-old. He was deteriorating.

Short Horror Stories Volume 3

Who knew how long he would be with her? Deciding it couldn't do any harm, she replied. Yes, they could meet but only at her home. She gave the name of the town but not a street address until there was confirmation. Whoever she was speaking to was obviously excited to meet Charlie and promised to board the next flight from Italy, meaning he would be with her by that evening. Miranda could do nothing but wait.

The relief and excitement of Charlie's presence was quickly turning to sadness, even fear. The more Miranda considered the future, the bleaker it all felt. Sure, he was back. But in what capacity? She tried to resist using the 'z word', Charlie was hardly shambling towards her and trying to bite. However, a life with him permanently five and forever watching cartoons was only marginally better than him being gone. Miranda felt a wave of guilt as the thoughts swept through her, but she couldn't deny they were how she really felt. Her loneliness would be ever-present, regardless of what happened next... unless her visitor could offer something more.

An email came through late afternoon to say the Italian, Marcos, had landed at London Gatwick. He'd be a couple of hours clearing the airport and another one at least on the train to Miranda's town. Nervous, she gave him the address and asked for him to get in touch again when he was near. She

146

P.J. Blakey-Novis

made more coffee, preparing for what she assumed would be a long night.

It was close to 9pm before the doorbell rang and Miranda was greeted by a man far younger than she had expected. Marcos couldn't have been more than thirty, athletically built but twitchy and anxious. In the moments it took to welcome the man into her home, he had glanced up and down the street several times. Miranda led him to the living room, Charlie still fixed in place.

"Charlie," Miranda said, reaching for the remote. "This is Marcos."

"Where's Daddy?" Charlie asked, looking around the room as though he had just remembered his father existed.

"He had to work away for a few days." This was the first thing that came to Miranda's mind and Charlie just shrugged, oblivious to the fact that Daniel's job never involved working away.

"Hello Charlie," Marcos said, his accent thick, his smile forced as he looked at the rotting boy before him. "Your mum was a bit worried about you. She said you had a bad dream?"

Charlie eyed his mother suspiciously.

"Can you tell Marcos about it, Charlie? He can help with bad dreams, so you don't have another one."

"I'm not tired so I won't dream," Charlie announced, reaching for the television remote. Miranda placed her hand on the black plastic first, flinching as Charlie's cold

Short Horror Stories Volume 3

skin landed atop hers.

"You will need to sleep soon," Marcos said. "Your mum said you haven't slept at all since you came back from the bad place. Can you tell me what it was like there?"

"Pretty," Charlie told him.

Miranda shot Marcos a look. "But Charlie, you said..."

"It looked nice. Green, like when we went camping. But the people were mean."

"What did they do that was mean?" Marcos asked.

"A man was hitting me. And shouting at me. I didn't like it."

"And someone rescued you?"

Charlie nodded.

"What did he look like?" Marcos asked.

"Scary at first. Then he pushed the bad man away and picked me up. Told the other children to follow us."

"And then you woke up?" Miranda asked. Charlie nodded. "Want more cartoons?" The boy nodded happily, even when Marcos ruffled his hair, causing large clumps to fall from his head.

In the kitchen, Miranda filled two mugs with black coffee and looked at the Italian with expectant eyes.

"And that is all he has said?" Marcos asked.

"Yes, but I don't know what it means. It seems to fit with what you believe though, right?"

"It does," the man replied, nodding, deep in

148

P.J. Blakey-Novis

thought.

"So what happens now? He doesn't even..." Miranda glanced through to the living room and lowered her voice. "He doesn't even know he's dead. How do I tell him that? And how do we tell everyone the truth? This is too huge to keep a secret!"

Marcos tapped his fingers on the table as though getting his words clear in his mind before speaking. "What is it you would like to see happen here?" he asked.

"I... I guess I want to know what will happen to Charlie. Do you know how long he will last? I certainly don't. He could be five forever or his body could fall apart within hours." Miranda felt herself close to tears, terrified of losing her only child all over again yet equally frightened of him staying the way he was.

"I'm afraid he will not remain for long, that is certain. Him being here, on this plane, is not how things are meant to be. Surely you understand that?"

"Of course he's not supposed to fucking be here!" Miranda hissed. "That's bloody obvious. But he *is* here. And he can help prove your theory. This could change the entire world! Imagine the effect reversing religion would have."

"You think people would believe you?" Marcos asked, eyebrows raised.

"You mean, us. People would believe *us*. This is your mission too. That's why you're here."

149

Short Horror Stories Volume 3

Marcos nodded, lost in thought. "Naturally. But we need more details from the boy."

Miranda was exhausted from a combination of shock at Charlie's return and the obvious lack of sleep. Wary as she was to entrust her child's safety to a stranger, she reluctantly agreed to take turns with Marcos in watching the boy. At first the Italian had laughed when Miranda asked if he thought Charlie could die twice, until he realised that she was serious.

"Death isn't a fixed thing, it appears," he had told her. "His body is failing, that much is clear. I suspect the physical being is just a housing for the boy's soul, and that, I can only speculate, would remain in some form or another when the body is gone."

"Could he take over another body?" Miranda asked incredulously. Her initial thoughts of horror movie possession tales made her shudder before an altogether brighter idea entered her mind. *He could take another child's body. I could pretend I've adopted. We could have a normal life.* She shook her head as though trying to physically push the idea away – where would she find a child's body for Charlie to dwell in? Could she force this heartbreak on another parent?

"I expect so," Marcos replied. "So we must be careful. You sleep, I will sit with Charlie. Perhaps with some time alone he will open up to me."

Miranda resented the idea that Charlie was

P.J. Blakey-Novis

withholding information from her but, whether that were true or not, she knew she needed sleep. They had agreed on three-hour intervals and she set an alarm on her phone, falling into her bed. She was fast asleep before her door was gently pushed open. Asleep before the shape of Marcos appeared at her bedside. Too tired to even feel the prick of the syringe.

Marcos took a seat beside Charlie and reached for the remote. The room was plunged into silence as he turned off the television, Charlie seeming to snap out of the trance the cartoons had held him in.

"Where's Mummy?" he asked, looking around. As he turned his head, the grey flesh on his neck tore, exposing tendons caked in black, dried blood.

"She's sleeping, Charlie," Marcos said, his gaze fixed on the boy. "Do you know how you got here?"

"I live here," Charlie replied, not understanding this stranger's question.

"You *used* to live here," Marcos explained. "And then you died. You drowned in the pond, do you remember?" Tears welled in Charlie's eyes and he shook his head. "And now you have come back, spreading lies about the afterlife." Marcos' jaw was clenched, spittle forming at the corners of his mouth. "Did you know it was wrong to lie?" he asked, voice filled with venom.

Charlie began crying in earnest, trembling

Short Horror Stories Volume 3

as rotten teeth chattered, some falling loose and dropping to the rug. "I... didn't... lie," he managed between sobs. "I want Mummy." Charlie tried to stand from the sofa but Marcos grabbed a cold arm, holding it tightly. Charlie struggled to free himself from the grip which, under normal circumstances, would have been impossible. However, the looseness of skin and muscle gave Charlie more flexibility, barely noticing the handful of flesh he left behind as he ran to Miranda's bedroom.

He couldn't wake his mother, no matter how hard he tried to shake her. He noticed her breath, slow and deep, and was about to scream out when a hand wrapped around his mouth from behind. Charlie found himself lifted off the floor and carried back to the living room, before being thrown roughly onto the sofa.

"Stay!" Marcos ordered. "Your soul should not be here, Charlie. This is the Devil's work. You must return to where you were sent by our Lord."

Charlie remained in place, too frightened to move, too young to understand anything more than a deep determination not to return to the bad place.

Marcos' gaze was fixed on the boy as he retrieved his briefcase from the kitchen table, opening it as he took a seat beside Charlie. "You will hurt you mother, Charlie," Marcos announced. "You will hurt everyone and ruin every*thing*. You don't want that, do you?"

P.J. Blakey-Novis

Charlie shook his head, more clumps of hair and scalp dropping from him.

"Then you must move on." Marcos pulled a rosary from the case along with a golden crucifix. He placed the cross onto Charlie's forehead, the skin so soft it left an imprint as Marcos began praying in Latin. The same phrase, one far beyond Charlie's understanding, repeated over and again. Charlie could feel a change coming over him, a weakening of his already destroyed body. A fading of the room around him, the house, the town... until he found himself in green pastures once more, an angry looking priest marching towards him.

Miranda awoke the following day, late into the morning. Her head felt groggy, almost hungover, and she panicked as she saw she had slept through her alarm by many hours. Flinging herself out of bed, she almost ran to the living room with the intention of apologising to Marcos. What she saw made her vomit across the rug.

Charlie's body remained on the sofa but appeared as though it had sunken in on itself. Tight greyish blue flesh was pulled across bones, as though someone had applied shrink wrap to a skeleton. Eyes stared at nothing, eyes which had died for a second time.

She found Marcos in the kitchen, drinking coffee and scrolling through his phone, not a care in the world. "What the fuck?" she

153

Short Horror Stories Volume 3

demanded, at a loss for any more words.

"We didn't think he'd last long," Marcos said with a shrug. "Probably for the best."

"For the best?" Miranda yelled. "He was my son! I thought you wanted to learn more, to discover the truth. You don't seem bothered at all!"

"This is something you'll just have to put behind you, I'm afraid. Charlie is gone. You got to see him one more time and you should appreciate that."

"What now?" Miranda asked. "How do we spread the word? People need to know the truth; the world needs to know the lies spread by the church."

"No, they don't," Marcos said. "You should forget all about this." He pushed his chair back and stood. Something about the way he was looking at her set Miranda on edge.

"I don't understand. This story, this evidence, is what you've been looking for. Isn't it?"

"It is... was. But Charlie's isn't the first case like this. It happens far too often. Always with children. Which is annoying, because I can't stand kids, you know." Marcos allowed himself a wolfish grin.

"I'm not following," Miranda admitted, taking a step back.

"Fuck. I was hoping you could just accept Charlie's passing and I'd be on my way. But fine, you want answers, I'll give you them. Just don't expect to like what you hear."

"I'm listening," Miranda said, taking

154

P.J. Blakey-Novis

another step back to increase the distance between herself and Marcos.

"What Charlie said, about heaven and hell and the Devil and so on, is pretty much the truth. But... as a Christian in the truest sense, my role within the church is to quash these kinds of stories. I mean, imagine it! There would be uproar, a huge loss in the number of people blindly following God, and in turn a huge drop in revenue."

"Revenue? You mean money?"

"Of course I mean money! The church is worth a ridiculous amount, as I'm sure you can imagine. Humanity's ignorance is astounding when you think about it. If God was really the good guy, and his followers actually cared about other people, don't you think that wealth would be used for something that benefitted mankind rather than private jets and megachurches?"

"You're evil!" Miranda squealed, hating how weak her voice sounded.

"I suppose," Marcos agreed. "It gets a bit muddly when things are reversed. I worship the bad guy, so I'm the equivalent of what most people think is a devil worshipper. But it's arguably worse than that, because it's under the guise of being *good*. You follow?"

Miranda did follow, all too well. Her ideas were correct, Charlie had been rescued from the hell that was heaven, but she, his own mother, had let this monster into their home.

"The world will know the truth," she vowed, turning to run.

155

Short Horror Stories Volume 3

Marcos was on her in seconds, his strong arms pinning her to the hallway floor. He didn't enjoy this part of his job but knew it was necessary. The chances of anyone believing the woman's seemingly crazy story were slim, but who knew what other people would come forward with similar accounts. Hands around her throat, Marcos found himself looking away as he applied pressure until he felt Miranda's body fall limp.

He followed protocol to the letter, stringing the woman up by the neck to mask at least some of the bruising he had left. A typed suicide note left on her open laptop screen detailed how the grief became too much to bear. Nothing anyone would be suspicious of. And like that, he was gone, the greatest lie in the world kept safely hidden for another day.

P.J. Blakey-Novis

Rise of a Fucking Superstar

Discretion has no place in the film industry. Why hide an act that everyone else is either doing or has no issue with? I certainly don't care about being seen as I place my diamond-encrusted compact mirror beside the sink in the lavish bathroom and unclip the capsule around my neck. I'm alone in the bathroom for now but it doesn't matter. I'm a fucking superstar.

The sound of metal on glass echoes as I tap out enough coke for a chunky line, one that I hope will see me through the next hour at least. I always save time (and reduce the risk of wasting any of the larger rocks) by grinding the powder as finely as possible in advance. Taking the silver-plated straw from the inner pocket of my clutch, I hoover up Colombia's finest and check my nostrils in the mirror above the sink.

Satisfied that I look presentable, I pack the paraphernalia away and strut back to my allotted table, the bitter taste of the drug dripping down my throat as I rinse with a glass of 1982 Krug. This is my first awards ceremony and I relish in the opulence of it all. It may be far from the Oscars, but I'm on my way up and I already know that this is my night as I listen to the nominees being announced.

I look towards the stage but I'm not really

Short Horror Stories Volume 3

focussing on anything other than the words as the names flow forth, most of which are entirely predictable. After what feels like an age, I hear "...and the nominees for Best Actress are...Oriana Charles for *Pandemonium...*" and I add a less than enthusiastic clap to the applause surrounding me.

"...Danni Thompson for *Mask of the Devil...*" (cue another half-arsed clap) "...Sarah McElmond for *Bittersweet...*" (I'm not even clapping once for that bitch) and "...Veronika Smith for *One Night in the Woods.*"

"Bastard," I mutter through a grin as I feel eyes fall upon me. I'd made it all-too fucking clear that my name is Veronika, just Veronika, nothing else and certainly not anything as mundane as Smith! You don't hear people ruining Beyonce's name with unnecessary extras, or Cher's, or Madonna's. These are the heights I'm climbing to and it's about time every one of these pricks realised it.

I empty the last of the champagne into my flute and down it, allowing a very unladylike burp to escape my mouth. I head back to the bathroom to powder my nose once more and check myself in the mirror. I look as fabulous as I feel and I wonder about the afterparty later, trying to decide who would be a suitable conquest to take home with me. It hadn't taken me long in this business to understand that every action, every decision,

158

P.J. Blakey-Novis

would affect my prospects. Whomever I go home with tonight will need to be someone successful, a winner of at least one category, and ideally married so they don't become too clingy. I decide that's a decision for much later and return to table 29 with the intention of feigning interest in the unavoidable speeches.

My God, this is dull, I think as Sloane bangs on about Sweet Little Chittering and the 'tragedy' that took place there. Yes, people died. Yes, some of it was pretty shocking. I'm not completely heartless. But it was just a freak occurrence in some inbred village. Out of the city, where things are usually a bit weird. *Although*, I realise, *there was that weird tower block thing too. And that was in the city. A shitty area, obviously, but still...*

As I listen to Sloane pretend to care about anyone other than himself, I'm pulled from my thoughts by the sound of chair legs squealing across the parquet floor. The chair next me, in fact – one which is supposedly reserved for my date. A chair I made the definite decision to keep empty. I look to see who would have the audacity to join me, expecting some sleazy producer to be trying his luck, but it is no-one I recognise. Sliding in beside me is a man much older than me, wearing a tailored suit and a black fedora, looking perfectly average. Not handsome, not ugly. Forgettable but not offensive to behold...for his age, which I'd put at mid-

Short Horror Stories Volume 3

sixties. Average in every way... apart from a flicker of orange in his eyes. He looks at me with a smile which I return, and I sense something which makes me uneasy, like he knows me. I mean, *really* knows me. Knows what I've done and how I got here.

I stand, grabbing the empty glass to clarify that I'm off to the bar, and pick up my clutch. Sloane is still waffling on about the village tragedy through the too-loud speakers, but I swear I can hear the older man say, "See you soon, Veronika." For a moment I panic, certain that something is off, but I put my sense of paranoia down to the coke. At the bar I opt for a large single malt and hover there for a moment, taking a few sips, reluctant to return to my seat. I know, however, that I have no real choice. When (not *if*) I win, I need to be sat where I'm expected to be.

"Good choice, Veronika," the man says with a grin as I take my seat. "Lagavulin is one of my favourites. You should try the thirty-year-old if you ever get the chance. It's to die for." I can't work out if it's due to the general volume in the room, but it sounds as though the man is hissing his S's, or maybe has a lisp.

"How do you know it's Lagavulin?" I ask, an eyebrow raised. I'm genuinely curious but not exactly afraid.

"I know all kinds of things about you," he replies and I roll my eyes at the cryptic comment. I decide that he most likely is just another sleaze, over-confident for his age, and return my focus to Sloane as talks about a charity single which we have to endure a live version of very soon.

"For example," the man whispers so closely to my ear that I can feel his breath, "I know about Daniel."

My heart skips a beat and the hand holding my glass begins to shake enough to rattle the ice floating within it. I take a second to compose myself without looking his way and raise the glass to my lips before responding.

"What is this?" I ask. "A shakedown?"

The man responds with a hearty laugh. "Goodness me! Not at all my dear, not at all. It's not my place to judge others but, for what it's worth, I think you did the right thing. You certainly deserve better than what he could offer."

"How do you know all this?" I ask, the coke and the alcohol barely concealing the fear that is rising from my stomach. "And what do you want?"

"I know lots of things, as I said. *How* I know them isn't really relevant. And as for what I want... we'll get to that later."

Putting on my best *I-don't-care* face, I meet his freaky orange eyes and tell him to leave, threatening to call security and have him thrown out. It seems the best response. I don't want a repeat of the Daniel incident but if I need to go that way to protect myself then I will.

Short Horror Stories Volume 3

I watch as some scantily clad assistant hands Sloane a pile of envelopes. I know what this means and wait for my name to be called and my life of fame and adoration to officially begin. The man beside me is still mumbling something but I ignore it – this is my moment.

"And the award for Best Actress goes to..." comes through the speakers. I hold my breath, despite knowing I will win. "Veronika Smith!" I push my chair out and begin to stand as the room is filled with applause. I try to look shocked at the result but the man in the black hat touches my arm, sending a jolt of electricity through me.

"Does it really count as winning if you curse your competition?" he asks. Now the shock on my face is genuine and I feel myself about to faint.

"Oops, looks like Veronika has had a few too many this evening," Sloane announces, causing an eruption of laughter all around me. *What a dick!*

I regain my composure and take a few steps towards to the stage to claim my prize. My legs feel heavy, my ears ring. *How did he know? Who, or what, is he?* The moment is stolen from me as I struggle to get to the stage. What should have been my moment of glory is now tainted by threats and confusion.

I collect my prize and only manage to mumble a thanks as Sloane fixes me with a bemused, smug look. "Anything else to add?"

P.J. Blakey-Novis

he asks, and I take a small bow before carefully stepping down from the stage. I take a few steps towards the bar before realising my clutch is still on the table. I glance in the direction of my seat and feel a sense of dread sweep over me as those orange eyes keep me in their sights.

I walk slowly and go to grab my bag when the stranger speaks one word with such authority that I do as I'm told without hesitation. "Sit."

"This song is pretty catchy," he says as the band starts up, completely ignoring my request. "You know, I've been told I can be a bit of an unpleasant character at times, but I don't think the *actual* spirit in the sky is any better."

I decide he's starting to ramble like a madman and try to block him out. What can he actually do to me? Daniel's death was an accident, as far as anyone is concerned, at least. Nothing to tie me to it and if they knew the details then they wouldn't believe it was even possible. *I'm safe,* I tell myself. *I'm a fucking superstar.*

"I need a drink," I tell him, unsure as to why I even said anything.

"Get two doubles, whatever costs the most," he tells me, sliding two fifty-pound notes across the table. "Then we will talk." I want to run, to get help, to somehow get away from this weirdo, but there is something more to this than just a sleazy guy or some lame blackmail attempt. The nagging

Short Horror Stories Volume 3

thought at the back of my head leaps forward with enough force to make my mouth open in surprise. *He has powers too.* Having little doubt that the man's abilities far exceed my own, I do as ordered and return to the table with two very large whiskeys just as the God-awful song finally ends.

"Now watch the stage," he tells me, leaning back in his chair and taking a gulp of his drink. There seems to be some confusion going on, with tech guys and security darting about and looking puzzled. After a few moments, England's darling actress Rebecca Cross is thrust onto the stage and it becomes clear they have lost Sloane.

"Where's Sloane?" I whisper.

"How would I know?" he replies, mocking innocence. "I've been here this whole time."

"I thought you knew lots of things," I say, pleased with my clever response.

"Touché. If you must know, he's with Daniel."

I feel my eyes bulge a little in shock and I don't even know where to begin with that piece of information. "How? Why? Who are you?" The words tumble from my mouth before he can even answer the first question. With a sigh, he places his glass on the table.

"How? His heart stopped. Why? I wanted to. I didn't like him. Not because he was a nasty person, nothing wrong with that, but because he thought he was so wonderful. If you want the truth, I didn't like the way he mocked you."

164

P.J. Blakey-Novis

This catches me off-guard, and I wonder what his intentions really are. I look to the stage and watch Rebecca try to keep things running smoothly but she's clearly not much use without a script to rehearse beforehand.

"And as for who I am," he continues, "let's just say I am aware of your powers."

"You're like me?" I ask, feeling some weird sense of camaraderie forming.

He laughs. "Hardly. I'm infinitely more powerful than you could ever be. But I've only met a few who can do what you have done so I wanted to meet."

"And what is it you think I have done?" I ask, noticing the slur in my voice for the first time.

"Hmm, let me see... tinkered about with old magic, cursed anyone who has threatened your chances of stardom, ruined people's careers.... oh, and murdered your boyfriend."

"I didn't murder anyone!" I hiss.

"Really? Then what would you call it? You did something which directly caused the death of another human. Is that not murder?"

I can't think of an answer, so I stay quiet and let him continue.

"As I said earlier, I do think he deserved it. Probably more than this Sloane character. But there was certainly some naivety on your part. I mean, sleeping with a producer just to get a role is beyond a cliché."

I feel my cheeks flush, blood rushing to my

Short Horror Stories Volume 3

head. I was a fool, I know that. But in this industry certain things are expected if you want to get anywhere. Look at Hollywood, for God's sake.

"I know," I say. "But I thought it was what was required. I didn't know he was fucking every actress he met."

"And that upset you enough for murder?" the man asks. "I think he got off lightly."

"You still haven't told me what you want," I say. "The evening is almost over. It looks like they are clearing the stage."

"No, my dear, the evening is just beginning." He clicks his fingers and the room is filled with a blaring alarm, guests look about in a panic, unsure if it's a drill or a real emergency.

Security begin ushering everyone outside and I slip my genuine fur coat over my shoulders. "Time to go, I guess," I say as the man rises.

"It seems that way. Would you do me the honour of escorting me to the after party?"

The question hangs in the air as I struggle to answer. I still want to run from this monster but part of me is intrigued. "Are you going to hurt me? Or kill me?" I ask and I mean it.

"No," he tells me. "Quite the opposite. I'm going to give you life."

The after party is packed as we step into the main room at the hotel. The dimmed lighting gives the place a debauched feel and

P.J. Blakey-Novis

I can just about make out a group of men passing a silver tray about, white lines glistening in the refection of the disco ball. It's largely standing (or dancing) room only but I'm desperate to sit. Somehow my date, for want of a better word, senses my discomfort and point towards one of three booths against the far wall. All of which are occupied but I follow him anyway.

He approaches a booth with one vaguely familiar man sitting in it. I search my memories for a name and decide on either Peter or Paul but I'm not certain enough to risk using either. Peter/Paul is grinning to himself, just sat holding his drink, and it's only when he sees us standing there that he lets out a yelp and fumbles with his belt buckle. In the darkness it takes me a moment to assess the situation, but it all becomes clear when Sarah McElmond crawls out from beneath the table, wiping at her cock-smeared lipstick. The pair scurry off, allowing us to sit.

"Classy joint," the man says.

"What's your name?" I ask.

"I have many," he replies, seeming to dodge the question. "Some real. Some just relating to the carcass I occupy. At the moment, most would call me Harris."

"And you're going to give me life?" I query.

"I do already have a life."

"Do you? What kind of life do you have? One where you need to cheat to win awards? One where you need to open your legs to get

Short Horror Stories Volume 3

a part? One that whizzes past in a cocaine and champagne filled blur until you're dead on a bathroom floor or your looks have faded to the point that not even the old creeps running the industry will stick it in you? If that's all you want from life, then you don't need me."

"I never said I needed you," I mumble.

"No, but you call yourself, and I quote, *a fucking superstar*, but what have you achieved on your own merits?"

He has me all figured out and suddenly everything feels wrong. I'm not a superstar, I'm just an ambitious tart and a mediocre actress. "So what are you suggesting?"

The glint in his creepy eyes is unmistakably devilish. "An alternative. Something similar, yet not the same. I want to make you a *genuine* fucking superstar."

"If I have to fuck you then that makes you no different," I point out, trying to be smart but failing miserably.

"You're not my type," he replies and wonder what actually would be. It's clear he isn't human, so my mind wanders briefly as I contemplate an angels and demons orgy. "My suggestion is that you use your powers to rise to stardom."

"You mean like I already have done? Did you not just call me out for cheating in the awards?"

"Like I said, my plan is *similar*. Your game, for this is all anything truly is, is to see just how far you can climb with the right tutelage.

P.J. Blakey-Novis

But without degrading yourself so much. Cheat, kill, ruin reputations, I don't care in the slightest. But you must always be the one on top, the one in control. If you wish to fuck, then do so, but only someone you want and let them pleasure *you* to get ahead. I can give you the ability to control decisions, influence the most powerful men and women, make you the most sought-after actress in the world."

"Why?" I ask, feeling myself getting caught up in his enthusiasm.

"For fun, I suppose. I've been around for a long time. I get bored easily."

"And the end goal?" I query, certain there has to be a target in mind, a height to reach.

"Hollywood, of course."

"You'll help me get to Hollywood, make me as successful as you're claiming, and what? Am I to be the face for your plans of movie domination because the world has seen enough of old white men running everything?"

"Drink up," he orders and I look to the table. The previous occupant has left half a bottle of cheap champagne in an ice bucket but no glasses. I take a swig from the bottle and weigh up my options.

"What will this cost me?" I ask, wondering how much would be too much.

"You need to let me enter you."

I fucking knew it! Disappointment washes over my face and I feel like walking out. All this conversation, the shaming me for my

Short Horror Stories Volume 3

behaviour, the promises of a career worth having, and he just wants to get his dick wet. I take another sip from the bottle and place it on the table.

"Okay," I say. What's one more unwanted lover? And at his age I'm sure it'll either be over quickly or he won't even be able to manage. He stays silent so eventually I look into his eyes. He's staring straight at me. He places his hands on either side of my head and I think he's about to kiss me. My stomach swirls with butterflies in anticipation. Does he want me right now? Right here?

"Thank you," he whispers, and I feel a jolt. The breath gets sucked out of me for a moment and I feel as though I am suffocating. Then I breathe, deeply, and I can hear him once again. "We should make a move."

The words sound different, closer. The man sits upright, still looking in my direction as his hands drop to his sides. His eyes glaze over.

I don't understand. The words were a thought, not spoken aloud, but he hears them.

Thank you for letting me in. We need to leave now before anyone notices Harris's situation. Bring the hat, though. I'm rather fond of it.

Before I realise what is happening, I'm stepping out from the booth and placing the black fedora on my head. Only I'm not. *He* is.

P.J. Blakey-Novis

He is still talking to me as we weave through the crowd and I'm unable to process what is happening. One of the men with the tray of coke grabs my arm and pulls me close as I pass him. He is about to speak but something in my eyes stops him, and he lets go.

Where now? I think, waiting on a response.

Home, comes the reply, *we have much to prepare for.*

Short Horror Stories Volume 3

Carver's Hill

According to the Internet, Carver's Hill is a hamlet in the south of England - a hamlet being defined as containing a population of less than one hundred and having no church. A church does exist, however, but certainly not in the Christian sense. When Carver's Hill was formed, in the late 1830s, nine families took residence on the land under the guidance of Christopher Carver – eighteen adults and eleven children. Basic stone homes were constructed, and the land was farmed, providing a peaceful way of life for the inhabitants. Almost two hundred years later and the same nine families live in Carver's Hill.

The descendants of each family now occupy the hamlet, having kept all marriages and reproduction amongst themselves since Carver's Hill was formed. The outside world would, most likely, frown upon what comes close to inbreeding, with the residents all now being related to one another in some way. The populace, however, see it as essential for keeping their tiny village pure.

Carver's Hill appears on no official maps as no roads run to, or through, it. It has no shops, no businesses of any kind. The people of Carver's Hill live off the land in much the same way that they did since the hamlet's creation. This is not to say, however, that

172

P.J. Blakey-Novis

they are unaware of the world beyond their piece of green land. They simply choose not to be a part of the larger community, and that community chooses to keep its distance.

Each week, at the building known as the Great Hall, Christopher Carver's only male direct descendant, Charles, leads what could be viewed as a religious service. The entire populace of Carver's Hill attend, without fail, and give thanks for their bountiful land. They begin by bowing their heads, muttering their words of gratitude to a higher power. Today's is a special meeting, coinciding with the first day of Harvest.

"Ladies and Gentlemen, children of Carver's Hill," Charles began, his booming voice filling the wooden building. The gathering falls silent, conveying their respect for their leader. "Today marks the first day of the Harvest, a celebration of both thanks and sacrifice." There were murmurs of agreement and excitement. "This is our one hundred and ninetieth year and we have never had to go without!" Charles almost shouted, his long beard bouncing as he spoke. The crowd cheered. "This afternoon, I need the heads of each family to come to see me so that I can assign your tasks for the festival. We have one week to get everything in order." The people that Charles referred to looked about at one another, exchanging smiles and nods of confirmation.

At the back of the Great Hall, seventeen-year-old Molly Alderson listened intently to

173

Short Horror Stories Volume 3

what was being said. She had been waiting for the Harvest celebration for many months, albeit for a different reason to the rest of the Carver's Hill residents. Molly's stomach flittered with a mix of nerves and excitement. *Risk and reward,* she told herself. *I'm taking a risk, but I have so much to gain. There's a whole world out there.* She felt a twinge of sadness as she looked at her father sat beside her. She was all he had after Molly's mother died in childbirth. As an only child, Molly was responsible for continuing the Alderson line; she was yet to understand how important, and non-negotiable, that would be.

As the meeting drew to a close, Molly's father, Daniel, pulled himself to his feet. Molly kept a hold of his hand. "Can I stay with you?" she asked, wanting to listen to the plans for the festival. "I can help with whatever Charles wants you to do."

"I don't see why not," Daniel replied, "As long as Charles doesn't mind. You're not a child anymore." He looked at his daughter fondly and Molly felt a moment of guilt pass across her. The congregation made their way from the Great Hall, leaving Daniel and the heads of the remaining seven families to talk with Charles.

"You don't mind if Molly sits in, do you?" Daniel asked, turning his attention to their leader. "She is next in line." Charles Carver smiled at Molly, sending a shiver up her spine. There was something off about this

174

P.J. Blakey-Novis

man that everyone seemed to adore but she couldn't quite place it.

"No problem at all," he said, before looking around at the others. "Thanks for staying behind," he continued, addressing the small group. "I thought it would be fair to mix up the tasks, so that you don't get lumbered with the same things each year. This will be Nathan's first year representing the house of Nightingale, following the sad loss of his father in the spring." There were a few muttered condolences at that point. "So, if you need any help, Nathan, don't be afraid to ask for it."

Charles reached into a small sack and retrieved some offcuts of cloth, each with an image on, before beginning to assign jobs. "Nathan Nightingale, you are responsible for setting out the tables for the feast. You'll need to check the condition of the tables we used last year and make any repairs which may be necessary." The young man nodded and took this as his cue to leave. "Joseph Northwood, bunting and decorations." A bearded man in his late fifties nodded, despite not appearing happy with his allocated task. "Eleanor and David Igden, I'd like you to prepare the fruit wines. There should be plenty in casks, but it will need bottling. If you can also check the levels of ale, that would be helpful. Matthew Brown, you're on preparation of the bread. Our numbers have reached almost sixty so we will need quite a few loaves. Jacob Argyle, you are

Short Horror Stories Volume 3

responsible for the gathering and preparation of fruit and vegetables. Margaret Lewis, you can help Jacob. Elsa Stewart, you are stuck with providing the music again this year. I hope you don't mind? You are the best person for the job," Charles said with a smile. Elsa appeared to blush, but nobody disagreed. Elsa was a talented musician and had provided music for the festivities with her homemade string instruments for the last twenty years.

"That just leaves us with the Aldersons," Carver said, looking again at Molly. "I'd like you two to prepare the meat for the feast. Take two pigs, and as many chickens as you feel will be required." Molly struggled to hide her distaste and Daniel quickly interjected.

"Molly has never prepared a carcass before," he explained. "Perhaps we could take a different task if she is to be helping this year?"

"Molly has asked to be involved, yes?" Carver asked Daniel, despite already knowing the answer. "So, I would suggest that it is time she learned what is required of her." Daniel squeezed his daughter's hand before she could respond.

"Of course, Charles." Daniel gave a quick nod and led Molly out of the hall.

"You know how I feel about the animals," Molly began, before they had even made it back to their house.

"Don't worry about it," her father replied.

P.J. Blakey-Novis

"I'll get it done. If Charles asks, then we'll just say I showed you. He'll be busy enough with his own tasks."

"What exactly does he do?" Molly asked, the question sounding much more disrespectful than she had intended. "I mean, I just wondered." Daniel's gaze shifted to his feet.

"Charles is the head of Carver's Hill. It's his responsibility to secure the Harvest offering."

"Which is what?" Molly asked, her curiosity piqued. "Is that what goes on when you and the others disappear after the banquet?"

"It's a solemn tradition," Daniel replied. "But it's also a secret one. When I'm gone, you will take my place as head of the Aldersons. Then you will be shown the Harvest offering."

"So, you really can't tell me any more than that?" Molly asked, surprised at her father's response.

"I'm afraid not, Molly. You know I hate to keep anything from you, but this is important. You honestly don't need to know yet, so you shouldn't worry."

"Hmm," Molly murmured. "Fine." *It doesn't matter what that secretive nonsense is about, anyway,* she thought. *That'll be my chance to leave this place for good.*

"Hey Molly." Molly heard her name being called and spun on her heels to find Nathan standing at the entrance to the barn.

Short Horror Stories Volume 3

"Oh, hey Nathan," she replied, trying to hide the smile that wanted to form. If she'd been completely honest, Molly would have admitted she'd had a crush on Nathan for the last couple of years. He seemed to have not noticed, however, or had chosen to ignore it.

"Charles asked me to come by to see how the meat prep was going?"

"Oh, yeah. It's all done," Molly said, neglecting to mention that her father had done all of the work.

"How did you do?" Nathan asked, a hint of suspicion in his tone. "I know you don't eat the meat." Molly paused, trying to form a believable response.

"I hated it," she replied. "But I did my duty." Nathan nodded, seeming to accept what he was being told. "So," Molly continued, changing the subject slightly. "Are you excited about tomorrow? It'll be your first time as head of your family. You even get to join in the secret activity at the end."

"Of course I'm excited," Nathan replied. "It's an honour."

"Did your father ever tell you what's required from you? After the festivities, I mean?"

"No, it's not for anyone to know until the time comes around."

"I know that, I just wondered. My father won't tell me what happens either," Molly said, "But I think it's something a bit weird. Last year he came back soaked in blood."

Nathan took a few steps closer to Molly

P.J. Blakey-Novis

before glancing back at the door. He leaned in, whispering almost conspiratorially. "I remember the blood from my father too. But I don't know any more than that and couldn't tell you even if I did. I'm sure it's just a ritual. They probably sacrifice a chicken and chant some of the old songs. Either way, you know it isn't our place to question it. Be careful who you talk to about this."

"I can't imagine it just involves some chanting," Molly said. "And he was soaked in blood."

"So?" Nathan retorted. "Whatever happens tomorrow evening will be an essential part of our survival here. It sounds as though you are questioning Charles' actions!"

"Of course not," Molly muttered, knowing that to continue would land her in considerable trouble. *I'll be out of here by the end of tomorrow; no need to worry about what goes on.*

"I'll see you at the feast," Nathan said, a smile now forming. Molly forced a smile in return, knowing that Charles had been checking up on her.

On the day of the feast, the whole hamlet of Carver's Hill was busy preparing. While tables were being set out in the Great Hall, bunting was being hung, and bread was being baked, Molly took advantage of everyone being occupied and stole away to her bedroom. Over the past few months, she had been busy making preparations of her

Short Horror Stories Volume 3

own. She had sewn a bag, large enough to contain her meagre belongings. She knew that she would be missed if she did not attend the feast, but this did not concern her. With no real knowledge of the world outside Carver's Hill, and none of the currency that the rest of the country used, it made sense to eat her fill before making her way into the world. She also hoped to make off with a few loaves of bread, if they could be taken unnoticed. Her only opportunity would be when her father was unable to check on her, and that would only be during the secret ritual as the festivities reached a close. Based on previous years, Molly estimated that she had almost an hour to make her escape.

The sun was still high in the sky and it was warm for an autumn day, so Molly decided to take a walk. Although the rest of her neighbours would have expected her to be contributing to the festival, as far as she was concerned her tasks had been completed, even if her father had done all the work. There was a stream which marked the northernmost edge of Carver's Hill and she wandered there, daydreaming about her adventures to come, pushing the guilt of abandoning her father to the back of her mind.

The stream bubbled and gurgled, almost peacefully. A few of the smaller, brown birds chirped in the trees. Molly could see why everyone thought of Carver's Hill as a paradise. *Perhaps I'll return one day,* she

P.J. Blakey-Novis

thought. *Maybe the outside world is a terrible place, but I must find out for myself.* Her thoughts were interrupted by a scream.

Instinctively, Molly ducked down low on the bank of the stream, listening out for any further screams. The voice did not sound familiar, and it had come from the other side of the stream, so no resident of Carver's Hill should be over there. A few moments passed before another scream shattered the tranquillity.

Molly was afraid for the first time in her life. In Carver's Hill there had never been a reason to fear anything, but this was new. Something bad was happening and she did not know what to do about it. Lowering herself further, so that she was almost face down in the grass, Molly tried to peek across the stream and into the field on the other side. At the far end there stood a line of trees and Molly was able to determine the source of the screams. A woman, dressed in brightly coloured Lycra, was now stumbling across the field, towards the stream. She looked behind her several times and, even from that distance, Molly could see how wide her eyes were with fear.

Molly remained as still as her body would allow, her eyes scanning the trees, expecting a monster to come running out from the shadows. She hadn't expected the monster to be so familiar. Launching himself from between two thick oak trees, his long beard flapping wildly as he gave chase, Charles

181

Short Horror Stories Volume 3

gained on the woman within moments. Molly watched in terror as she saw their leader shove the woman from behind, knocking her to the ground. She could make out his arms moving rapidly as he rained down blows on the woman's face. Molly's stomach clenched, a feeling of sickness coming over her. She thought she knew what was coming next as she watched Charles straddle his victim. When the second figure emerged from the trees Molly let out a gasp. She quickly covered her mouth, certain that it had been loud enough to have been heard, but the two men showed no sign of having been interrupted.

Daniel approached Charles and the woman, seemingly reluctant to do so. Molly watched as Charles lifted the woman, his hands under her armpits, and wondered if she were dead or merely unconscious. Disbelief hit her hard as her ever-loving and kind father grabbed the woman by her ankles and helped Charles carry her towards the village.

Molly stayed as still as possible, waiting for the men to disappear from sight, and then waiting for another half hour to be sure they had gone. Now, more than ever before, Molly knew that she needed to leave Carver's Hill.

Molly's heart did not stop thumping until she was back in her room, her bag as ready as it could be. She considered leaving then and there, wondering how far she could get before anyone noticed. *I'll need food,* she

P.J. Blakey-Novis

thought. *And if I'm not at the feast then the whole village will be looking for me. If I wait, they may not notice until the morning.*

Molly considered confronting her father. What she had seen had shocked her to her core, but he was still her father; surely, he had a good reason for what he had done. Charles frightened Molly, even more so now, but she did not fear Daniel. He had not looked as though he wanted to be in that field, carrying that poor woman. If he knew his daughter had seen him then perhaps he would feel the need to explain his actions. *Or perhaps I don't know him at all?*

Once Molly had regained her composure, she made her way out into the street. As hard as she tried to look innocent and 'normal', she felt far from it. Something unpleasant had happened, something unexpected, and there was a dark secret at play in Carver's Hill. Worse still, her own father was involved with it. As she rounded a corner, Molly walked straight into Elsa Stewart.

"Molly!" Elsa exclaimed. "How are you, my dear? Excited for this evening?"

"Of course," Molly replied, putting on a smile. "Erm, you haven't seen my father, have you?"

"I think he's with Charles," Elsa said, looking uneasy. "They have a lot to prepare so it may be best if you leave them to it." With that, Elsa hurried away, and Molly had no doubt that whatever was happening with that woman, Elsa knew about it.

183

Short Horror Stories Volume 3

Making her way to her father's barn, Molly prepared her excuses for bothering him. She could think of nothing plausible other than asking to be assigned another task for the festival, feigning boredom or some desire to be more involved. She did not make it inside the barn.

As she approached the large wooden doors, they swung open to reveal her father and Charles Carver. Charles' hands were bloody, his knuckles scraped and swollen. Molly's father was wearing the apron he used to prepare the meat and it was dripping with crimson. Molly took a breath and plastered a smile to her face as she approached the men.

"Hey," she said. The two men looked at her before Charles moved to close the barn doors.

"Hey Molly," Daniel said. "What are you up to?"

"Not a lot," Molly lied. "I wanted to see if you needed any more help." Charles kept his distance at the barn door, as if guarding it.

"I think we have it all under control," Daniel said with a smile as he pulled the apron off. "Just finished up with the meat for tonight." *You told me you'd done it all yesterday,* Molly thought, struggling not to say it aloud, settling for an 'okay', instead. "Come on. I need to get cleaned up and we can head out for the feast." Daniel gave Charles a curt nod and took Molly's arm, leading her back to their home.

"Do you want to sit with me, at the head

184

P.J. Blakey-Novis

table?" Daniel asked. Molly couldn't hide her surprise. The head table was reserved for the representatives of the nine families, plus their spouses if they had them. Never had anyone else been allowed to dine there. "Charles suggested it," Daniel said.

"Well, I suppose that I should then," Molly replied, knowing that if the idea had come from Charles then it wasn't open to negotiation. Something niggled at Molly, something more than nerves about her plan to leave Carver's Hill, something connected to what she had witnessed that afternoon. *Did my father see me?* Molly doubted it; her father would have told her if he'd seen her. Then a far more terrifying thought came to mind. *Had Charles seen me? Did he know that I'd watched him attack that woman? What would he do about it?* Being offered a place at the head table was certainly unusual and seemed to follow a series of unusual events. Tonight wasn't going to be a typical Harvest feast.

Molly did her best to keep her thoughts on the festivities, enjoying the freshly made breads and fruit. Her reluctance to eat meat was well known, and Daniel ensured she had enough of the other items available. Despite everything that had happened that day, Molly was determined to enjoy these last moments with her father. She knew that, as soon as the feast was over, Daniel would be led to the chambers at the back of the Great Hall, and

Short Horror Stories Volume 3

she would finally have the opportunity to leave.

The group chatted around the table, about nothing of any real importance. The bottles of fruit wine went down quickly, as did the ale. Raucous laughter filled the hall as everyone enjoyed the festivities. Even Molly, despite everything, began to relax. Until Daniel began to spasm.

Molly had been in conversation with Nathan, talking about his plans to take a wife, when she felt a hand grab at her side. Turning to face her father, she watched as his head tipped back, foamy, bloody spittle appearing from his mouth. Matthew and Jacob leapt to Daniel's aid and the laughter in the Hall turned to screams. Molly could only watch as her father fell to the ground, twitched several times, and fell still. The only person who did not move, or show any surprise at Daniel's sudden demise, was Charles.

Molly dropped to her knees, cradled her father's head, and sobbed. The rest of the villagers stood silently, a combination of shock and sadness overcoming them. Eventually, Charles Carver stood, commanding the room's attention.

"People of Carver's Hill," he began, clanging two goblets together. "We appear to have lost a beloved member of our clan." Molly was sure she could see a smirk appear at the corner of Charles' mouth. "As distressing as this is, I beg of you all not to let it ruin the

P.J. Blakey-Novis

festivities. We owe it to the higher powers that we honour them in this way. Tomorrow we can mourn. Today is for celebration." Molly couldn't believe what she was hearing, taking to her feet in front of Charles. Before she could speak, the leader of Carver's Hill fixed his gaze on her. "Molly Alderson. You are now the head of the Alderson family. We have never had anyone so young join these sacred ranks. Tonight, both you and Nathan, will take part in the sacred ceremony for the first time."

A cheer erupted from the neighbouring tables and Molly simply stood, overwhelmed by what was happening. Her father was gone, presumably poisoned, and her best opportunity to escape had been thwarted. *This is no coincidence,* Molly thought, resuming her place at the table. *Charles knows I was there. He needs me to be at the ceremony and that can only happen if my father is gone. Charles is a murderer and a monster.*

Molly grabbed a goblet of wine and swallowed it down in one breath. She took to her feet, tears streaming down her cheeks and looked Charles in the eye.

"I'll have no part of it!" she yelled. Again, shock descended upon the room. "I don't want to go to your secret ceremony, and I don't want to be head of my family. I want my father!" Molly only just managed to resist accusing Charles of murder before she turned to leave.

Short Horror Stories Volume 3

Molly had taken no more than four steps from the table before she felt strong arms around her waist, lifting her from the ground. Kicking her legs wildly, she tried to fight against him, but Charles was too strong. No one tried to help her; no one was willing to defy their leader. Molly found herself being carried through the ornate door to the rear of the Great Hall, where she was forced into a chair.

The room smelled sweet, as though incense had been burning. Charles ordered her to stay and Molly knew better than to ignore his order. She watched as Charles moved around the room lighting candles and she was finally able to see what was contained within the room that so few were ever allowed to enter. Once her eyes had adjusted and Molly's brain had processed what lie before her, she vomited.

The room featured candles adorning the walls, as well as nine heavy-looking robes which were evenly spaced on wooden hangers. Eight of the robes were white, the last one being red. Molly assumed, correctly, that the red robe belonged to Charles. In the centre of the room stood a stone table with an unfamiliar language carved around its edges. None of this came as a surprise to Molly, for she knew that the ceremony involved giving praise to a higher power. What she hadn't expected to see, the reality of which she was struggling to process, was what, or rather who, was on the table.

188

P.J. Blakey-Novis

Even without her brightly coloured running clothes, or in fact any clothes, Molly instantly recognised the woman. Her blonde hair stuck to her face with a mix of sweat and blood, eyes swollen closed, nose at an unnatural angle. There was a gap of around two inches between the woman's head and her neck, where it had been removed. Molly found herself thankful that the eyes were not left open.

The corpse had been laid out on the table in pieces; pieces which were in the correct places despite having been separated from one another. Arms had been removed at the shoulders; hands stolen from the wrists. The body had been halved at the waist, with each foot taken off at the ankle. Molly vomited again.

"We find ourselves in a bit of an unusual situation, Molly," Charles began.

"You killed my father," she spat.

"You saw something that you shouldn't have. I'm afraid this was my only option. Now you are the head of the Aldersons. Now you must partake in the ritual."

"And if I refuse?" Molly asked, wondering what Charles would actually do. Sure, he'd killed people, but he'd also been clear that she was now the head of the Aldersons, with no descendants of her own. For as long as Molly could remember, the fact that there were nine heads of nine families was essential. She had never really understood why; it was just the way things were. The one

Short Horror Stories Volume 3

question she needed an answer to more than anything popped into her head – *Could Carver's Hill continue with only eight families? If not, then I'll be allowed to live, at least.*

"I'm afraid you can't refuse, Molly. I'm truly sorry that it has come to this. You are the only one who can fulfil your role within our community. At least, until you produce a child. We can talk further tomorrow, but for this evening I, we all, need you to take part in the ceremony. It's the only way to protect our way of life."

"I don't want to," Molly said, quieter now. "Father was all I had."

"You have no choice. The ceremony will begin within minutes. The others will guide you through it. Do I need to restrain you?" Molly shook her head. *I'll sit through whatever ghastly offering they intend to make but I'll be gone by dawn.*

As if they had been awaiting their cue, the remaining seven entered the chamber and silently put on the robes. Charles took his red robe and Nathan passed one of the white robes to Molly, an apologetic look on his face. He glanced between Molly and the dismembered woman lying before them. If he was surprised by the gore-laden offering, then he hid it well. Molly remained silent, knowing she had no way out, and slipped the gown over her head.

"We have two new members this evening," he began. The others nodded their approval. "And because of this, I'll be explaining our

P.J. Blakey-Novis

ceremony as we go. As always, it is imperative that nobody interrupts me." At this point Charles looked at Molly. "We begin with a prayer, followed by the sacred vows."

Charles led the group in prayer as they held one another's hands, forming a circle around the morbid table. All heads remained bowed until Charles had finished.

"I shall begin with the vows," Charles explained, "moving to my left. That way Molly and Nathan will have heard them enough times to be able to repeat the words when necessary." There was a pause as Charles looked up to the ceiling.

"Oh generous one, oh ancient one, we are gathered before you again on this most sacred of evenings, vowing our allegiance to you. I, Charles Carver, give myself over to you completely. I promise to help lead Carver's Hill in honour of you, and I bring you this sacrifice."

The words were repeated by David Igden, who stood to Charles' left, followed by Joseph, Matthew, Elsa, Jacob, and Margaret, before it was Nathan's turn. He had memorised the words perfectly and uttered them with respect. Molly was torn, not wanting to go along with this insanity but arguing to herself that they were just words. *What harm can it do?* she pondered. Quickly, she recited the vow.

A moment's silence was interrupted by a loud clap of hands, followed by murmured chatting among the group. The whole

Short Horror Stories Volume 3

atmosphere had shifted from solemn to relaxed and caught Molly off guard. She looked to Charles, who now had his back to the group. He appeared to be pulling something from a small wooden box that Molly had not noticed on the floor. Something shiny. When Charles turned back to face the table, Molly understood what was to happen. She swallowed down hard as her mouth filled with bile.

"As you can see," Charles began, his attention focused on Nathan and Molly, "we have nine pieces of this fine offering."

"Ten," Molly said, defiance in her tone.

"Ten," Charles said with a smirk. "Well done. If you'd let me finish? We have nine pieces of this fine offering, plus the head. The head is the most sacred and is reserved for the ancient one. The remaining *nine* pieces are, of course, for each of us. Our reward, if you like, for our loyalty. David..."

Charles passed the shiny objects to his left, handing David Igden the long two-pronged fork and a carving knife. Molly watched in horror as David took a slice from the woman's forearm and slipped it into his mouth. The utensils moved on and Molly found she could not look away as pieces of flesh were taken from hands, legs, and feet. Nathan looked nervous as his turn came about, but it didn't stop him from slicing away a thin strip from the side of the woman's right hand. He placed it in his mouth and began chewing, his expression changing from one of reluctance to one of joy. Molly watched a little saliva drip down his chin, now pink with blood. Nathan handed Molly the knife. She held it in her trembling hand, bile trying to force its way out of her mouth.

"I don't even eat chickens," she pleaded, looking to Charles. "Please, I can't do this."

"Very well," Charles replied, causing puzzled expressions from the rest of the people. "I will help you." Molly took a step backwards.

"I'm here. I'm doing my part, with the prayers and the vows. I just can't do...that," Molly said through tears.

"Which is why I said I would help you," Charles explained, stepping closer to her. He put out his hand to receive the utensils. "The knife please Molly."

A rush of thoughts went through Molly's head at that moment, ideas of stabbing Charles, even cutting her own wrists in defiance. Her hands, however, seemed to act on their own accord, and passed the knife over to their leader. Charles leaned forward, placing one hand on the severed arm to hold it in place, while he sliced with the other. The whole time his eyes didn't look away from Molly. Plucking a sliver of pale skin between his fingers, Charles lifted it towards Molly.

"Open," he ordered. Molly glanced around at the others, willing someone to intervene, but they did not. She looked at the meat, grateful that it was a small piece. *Could I*

Short Horror Stories Volume 3

swallow it in one? Molly wondered. *I don't think I can chew it.* Reluctantly, she opened her mouth.

Molly had expected to gag. She had been certain that vomit would fly from her mouth as soon as that raw flesh hit her tongue, and she knew there would be nothing she could do about it. What Molly hadn't expected was the taste which filled her mouth. It was heavenly and she understood why Nathan's face had lit up so. She opted to chew, and the pink juices coated the roof of her mouth, leaving the wondrous flavour to linger. Her entire perspective had changed in an instant. She was no longer revolted by the dismembered woman lying before her. A moment of clarity had hit home. and she found Charles smiling at her.

"How is it?" Charles asked.

"It's wonderful!" Molly replied. "Chicken and pork I can do without quite easily but this is unlike anything I've ever tasted. It's pure, it's indescribable. What happens to the rest of it?"

"On this special night, we can eat as much of our allotted portions as we choose. Whatever is left will go to the pigs. The head is burned as an offering to the old and ancient one."

Molly didn't need to be told any more. She lifted the arm from the table and sank her teeth into the flesh. The rest of the group laughed, happily, as they tucked into their pieces of flesh. With that one taste, Molly

P.J. Blakey-Novis

understood everything. She felt a connection with the higher power, a responsibility for Carver's Hill, a desire to serve. Most importantly, all thoughts of leaving the hamlet had gone.

This evening she would feast and tomorrow she would bury her father. She made a mental note to ask Charles what poison he had used. If the flesh was untainted then perhaps she'd allow herself a little taste before saying her final goodbye. Her mind already began wandering on to Daniel's deliciously fleshy thighs.

Blurred and Fractured Memories

A fist to Lucy's nose split it, causing a torrent of blood. She staggered but kept on her feet...for a moment. The second punch landed her on her back in the filth of the alleyway. Eyes full of water, she couldn't clearly make out the figure standing over her but there was something familiar about the way he held himself. She went to let out a scream but was silenced by a wide blade being rammed into her mouth, splitting her cheeks. Rough hands grabbed at her, dragging her to a sitting position against the damp wall. The pain was too much, and she passed out as her attacker removed her eyes. She never felt the slice of the blade across her throat.

I was sixteen when I found the first body. Sixteen on that day, in fact. I'd spent the evening at the park with some mates, smoking weed and drinking shit lager. I'd started on my way home, feeling great, but something pulled me down that alley. Not physically, it was more like a command. Hard to describe – in my head but not *my* thought. She was propped up against the wall, empty crisp packets and other shit all around her. I remember thinking it was some girl who'd had too much to drink but that thought passed almost instantaneously.

P.J. Blakey-Novis

Even in the darkness of that piss-soaked alley, I could make out the pool of blood surrounding her. As I approached, heart now racing, I realised that her hoody was not supposed to be the sickening red that it now was. I crouched before her, listened for the sound of a breath, heard nothing. Stoned and drunk, I thought nothing about touching the body and how it would look to the police. Gently, I placed a hand under her chin to raise her head, before falling back and vomiting down the jacket I'd only received that morning.

The blood coating her hoody was from the gaping wound across her neck and that in itself would have been a gruesome find. But her face... She could have passed for *The Joker* with what looked like a crimson grin, only this was not down to makeup or face paints. Someone had cut from the corners of her mouth, tearing the flesh all the way to her ears. Blackened pits sank into her face where eyes should have been, and her nose looked as though it had met with a fist more than once.

I left her there. I mean, I thought about calling the cops, an ambulance, any-fucking-body, but I was a drunk teenager with a pocket full of drugs. So, I went home. My high got all fucked up after finding her like that and I started seeing things that night. White, pupilless eyes. Blackened teeth. Flickering images of bloody metal knives.

The next day, it was already on the news

Short Horror Stories Volume 3

before I could drag myself out of bed. Mum brought a coffee to my room, something that had never happened before, and told me they'd found Lucy in an alley. Murdered.

"Lucy?" I asked, processing. It hadn't looked like Lucy, but then it was just a mutilated body in the dark and I could hardly see straight anyway.

"She was a friend of yours, wasn't she?" Mum asked as I sat myself up. I'm sure she knew Lucy had been more than a friend on several occasions. That girl could suck the ocean through a straw. I would have been up for an actual relationship if she hadn't been fucking everyone I knew.

"Kinda," I mumbled, reaching for my phone. I needed to call the boys I was with last night to see if they'd heard.

Death follows me and I have seen it. It's been more than two years since I found Lucy's body. One year since Mum kicked me out for using again. I tried to get help, to get clean, but those fucking eyes are everywhere. The drugs are the only things that knocks me out enough so I don't see them. Down every darkened path, white eyes, blackened grin. I don't blame Mum at all, she really did try. Who'd want to live with a nasty junkie anyway?

It's pretty rare to find a dead body, ever. So the fact that I've found seven in such a short timeframe looks beyond suspicious. Found seven, reported none. Everything is a haze

P.J. Blakey-Novis

and I spend my nights in this run-down warehouse with other scumbags like myself. People have died here but I don't count those. They were just overdoses, self-inflicted.

Did I know any of the dead women aside from Lucy? I have no idea. I wouldn't have known it was Lucy if it wasn't for the news. There has been talk of a serial killer since the second girl was found, throat cut, eyes missing, that blood-soaked grin forced on her face. I was first to find them all, as far as I know, but remember nothing clearly. I felt guided there and I shudder to think about it – to think about Death and the hold it has on me.

I wonder if seven is the right number. I can't think straight. Could it be more? Was it just Lucy and my mind is reliving that night like some form of PTSD? Who said there was a serial killer? Was that just in my head? I can't follow my own thought processes, so I cook up one last hit and collapse on my filthy mattress.

I sleep soundly, numb and oblivious to my surroundings. But I awaken to a nightmare. Daylight streams through broken windows. I have no concept of the time but the first thing I notice is the smell. It's as though an entire football team has taken a shit next to where I lay. I pull myself onto my elbows, bloodshot eyes glancing around the grim building. I spy four bodies scattered about – nothing unusual with that. These fuckers tend to pass out anywhere. But they aren't

Short Horror Stories Volume 3

usually laying in bloody heaps of viscera.

I roll off the mattress, focussing on my breathing to stop myself throwing up. I take a few unsteady steps towards the closest body, a malnourished mess of a woman I knew as Sandra. Curled on her side, her hands were clasped against her abdomen as though she were trying to hold her guts in place. The knotted mass of intestines, blood, and shit suggested she'd been unsuccessful. I checked her face – eyes still where they were supposed to be. A different killer?

I moved my gaze to another body, a man who could have been anything from twenty to fifty years old. Slices in his arms, legs, and shoulder glistened red in the sunlight that poured though. He was face-down, and I had no intention of moving him so could only assume he'd bled out.

The remaining two had met the same end, slashed and gutted but their faces left intact. I felt no sadness at their passing, just more confusion. Who had done this, I didn't care to know. Why I was spared the same grisly end, was starting to trouble me.

I knew I had to leave, to get as much distance between the slaughter and myself as possible. For once, I was grateful my worldly possessions all fitted in one small bag. As I patted down the corpses for any cash or drugs that they would no longer be needing, I felt something move in my peripheral vision. Just a slight movement, like a branch moving in a breeze or a curtain twitching.

P.J. Blakey-Novis

But it's daylight? It seemed as though each day brought a new level of confusion. Death had never come to me without the cloak of darkness. I didn't know it even could. Yet, I sensed it. I have no doubt that, should I have looked up, my gaze would have been met by perfect white spheres and a cracked, blackened smile. But why would I want to see that?

Snagging a few coins and a small bag of what looked like MDMA, I threw them into my backpack. I got on my knees, shoving my stinking mattress across the floor to retrieve my prized possession. The one thing that meant more to me than my stash – a photo of me and Mum. It wasn't the only thing secreted beneath those rusty springs.

I had come to accept a level of confusion and put it down to my addiction. I didn't like it, but it was better than the alternative of seeing Death everywhere I went. As I looked at a very recently used machete, I wondered again why I had been spared. How had someone been brave enough to put it *under* me without fear of me waking? Was I being framed?

I took the weapon without much thought, managing to hide it in the folds of my oversized coat. I knew if I got caught with it then I'd be fucked, but I was certain someone was after me. Fucking with me. People were being butchered wherever I went – I was the common denominator in the killings yet could not understand why.

Short Horror Stories Volume 3

I left the squat in a hurry, almost running to the station. I managed to bunk a few trains until I was a good fifty miles from that shit-stinking hovel. I needed somewhere to shelter, somewhere I could shoot up and not be bothered by Death's fucking grin. And that was when I met Catherine.

It was a horrible evening, rain pelted down and all I could do was huddle in a shop doorway. I didn't know the area, I saw no other homeless people. The town was small, quiet, almost deserted.

"Are you okay?" I heard someone ask and I looked up to see a beauty before me. Maybe in her late twenties, long blonde hair, manicured hands gripping tightly to an umbrella. "It's not a night for sleeping outdoors."

"I'm used to it," I said, trying to force a smile.

"Well, you shouldn't have to be. I'm Catherine." Then she did something that nobody had done in more than a year. She offered me a hand. I felt awkward as I shook it, conscious of the filth encrusting my skin, but she either didn't notice or didn't care.

"Ben," I lied, trying desperately to get my thoughts to process clearly.

"Well, Ben, how about you come with me? I've got a spare room, a hot shower, and plenty of food."

"What's the catch?" I asked, immediately regretting it.

P.J. Blakey-Novis

Catherine looked offended for a moment before her smile reappeared. "No catch, just trying to do my good deed. I only mean for tonight. Perhaps you can find a hostel or something tomorrow? I probably wouldn't have offered if the weather wasn't quite so awful. But it's your choice, I'm only a couple of roads over."

"Thank you," was all I could manage, and I truly meant it. Tears welled in my eyes at the act of kindness I never expected to receive and, as we walked to Catherine's small apartment, I did my best to ignore the feeling of being watched by Death's white eyes.

Catherine unlocked the door to her apartment and walked in, kicking off her shoes and hanging her wet coat on a peg beside the door. I followed her in nervously. Something felt off about the whole situation, more than just the novelty of being shown kindness. I had no doubt that the night would end badly for one of us and I found myself hoping that, if one of us was to suffer, it would be me.

"Don't take this the wrong way," Catherine said as she moved into the open-plan kitchen. "But would you mind using the shower before anything else? I have some clothes you can wear once you've cleaned up."

"Someone else lives here?" I asked, then cursed myself. That sort of question is going to make her worry about my intentions,

Short Horror Stories Volume 3

surely. "I mean, the clothes?"

"Just me," she replied, eyeing me with a hint of suspicion. "Ex-boyfriend left some bits. They were for the charity shop anyway so you can have what you like. Bathroom is at the end of the hall."

I nodded and made my way through, locking myself in the bathroom. My perpetual confusion was worsening as I turned on the shower. Why was I here? What was Catherine really after? Why could I not outrun those bastard white eyes? How had Death followed me all this way?

I tried to shut off the incessant noise inside my head and at least attempt to enjoy my first shower in several months. I must have been in there for longer than expected as I heard banging on the door, Catherine calling to see if I was okay.

I shut off the water and stepped out, taking a towel from the back of the door and telling her I was almost done. I thought about shooting up, the shakes and sweats telling me that I couldn't hold off much longer. I dried my body, then used the towel to clear steam from the mirror so I could see what state I was now in.

What I saw frightened me enough to take a leap back, trip over my dirty clothes, and land with a crash. White, pupilless eyes. Black, cracked teeth. Skin that looked like fucking charcoal, all broken and covered in ash. A monster. Death itself. Me.

"No," I mumbled, trying to piece everything

P.J. Blakey-Novis

together. The bodies, that gruesome fucking carnage, that wasn't me. I'd found them, I hadn't killed anyone. Someone planted the bloody machete. Or did they? Gradually, as I lay on that stranger's bathroom floor, events began to fit together.

Lucy. I'd known her. I'd loved her, as much as a sixteen-year-old could love anyone. She was fucking around with everyone. I didn't like that. I don't remember killing her. I'd remember, wouldn't I? The others. Were there others? It's all too confusing. The junk keeps Death away...or does it just make me unable to strike again? Holy fuck! I don't understand. I need to leave.

I stand, wrapping the towel around my waist and unlocking the door. Catherine is on the other side, concern turning to fear. She screams but I can't understand why. She starts to run. I'm supposed to be getting the clothes, but I find myself chasing her. The machete is in my hand. When did I pick that up? I can see why she's screaming. I call her name, or at least try to. It doesn't come out right. It sounds like I'm snarling or growling. Poor woman is terrified, and I can understand why, I just can't stop.

She throws herself over her couch, rolling across the small living room floor. There is nowhere for her to go, and she knows it. I look at the black screen of the television mounted on the wall and can make out my reflection. Death's reflection. Rage builds to a crescendo. Anger at what I've become. Anger

Short Horror Stories Volume 3

at my own confusions and weaknesses. Anger at Catherine for putting herself in harm's way – in *my* way.

I stroll around the sofa, arguing with myself. I don't want to hurt her. My actions are not my own. I focus on one thought, just one. I will my arm to move and put the machete down, hoping that Catherine will grab it and end me. My arm moves, but too quickly, too violently. Catherine screams as I take a slice from her leg, the blade skimming the surface and removing a thin layer of skin. She tries to back away from me but has nowhere to go. Three more steps and I'm on top of her.

I hear myself tell her to smile but have no idea where that notion came from. I witness the horror as I ram the machete into Catherine's screaming mouth, slicing both cheeks open. She tries to scream but it comes out as a bloody gurgle. I dig out her eyes and throw them in my mouth, swallowing them virtually whole. She's close to unconscious now as fear, shock, and blood loss take a grip on her. At this point I see there is no going back and swipe the machete across her throat, ending it.

I wake up in a fresh-smelling bed for the first time in more than a year, after the best sleep I can ever remember. On the bedside table is the usual paraphernalia so I know I shot up last night, but I still feel well rested. Clean. Fresh. Like I'm at the start of a new

P.J. Blakey-Novis

beginning. I try to remember the name of the woman who offered me a roof and a shower. Katie? Cath? Kaitlyn?

I pull myself out of the wonderful bed and realise I'm naked. I don't see my clothes on the floor so try to creep to the bathroom to find a towel at least. The last thing I want is to frighten my Good Samaritan by walking around with my cock out.

The bedroom door creaks as I open it. I glance down the hallway and my hairs stand on end. Something is wrong. Again. Ignoring my nudity, I take cautious steps towards the living room. I see the machete, fresh blood coating the blade. I see *her*. I vomit. Memories of Lucy come back, blurred and fractured. It's too much of a coincidence. I see it all, every act of violence, as both parts of me collide. The monster takes control. I am Death. Only Death. And I will not stop.

Short Horror Stories Volume 3

We Want to Sing You a Song

White male. Early forties. Lives alone. I guess I fit the profile for a serial killer. But I'm not. Serial killers commit their crimes regularly, deliberately. I made mistakes. I drank too much. It wasn't my fault... I didn't know what I was doing... I had no control over my actions.

Excuses, ones I tell myself daily because I can't take responsibility for my own fuck-ups. I disgust myself sometimes as I sit alone, sulking like a child about how messed up my life has gotten. As if someone had forced the all the bourbon down my throat. As if someone had made me spend every penny of my wages on drink instead of the bills. As if I could expect Jenny to stay with me after I totalled our car, or disappeared for days on a bender, or forgot our wedding anniversary. As if I deserve any better... as if.

Of course all that shit should have been a wake-up call to clean myself up. Check into rehab (Jenny tried to make me because she did love me, but I refused because I'm a prick like that), sort my life out, make amends. But self-pity won and now I just drink alone, never speak to anyone, moping like the pathetic shite I've become. Each time I'm throwing my guts up I swear I'll stop, and sometimes I make it to lunchtime without a beer. My record is twenty hours but only

208

P.J. Blakey-Novis

because I slept through most of that. Could try for a New Year's resolution but first I need to get through fucking Christmas. It's a horrible time of year as it is, so there's no fucking way I'm taking on that without a drink.

December 20th, I noted with a glance at the calendar. A calendar just full of blank squares, symbolic of my ambition and intentions, I guess. I looked to the clock. 5.45pm. I could see both time and date from my position on the living room floor which has long been my bedroom, a half-deflated air mattress barely keeping me off the thin carpets. It was dark outside and almost just as dark inside. I must have been sitting there for a while so I reached for a lamp, knocking half a can of yesterday's cider over. It only added to the room's smell but barely made a difference.

And then it happened.

For the first time in what must have been weeks, the doorbell rang. So unexpected, I literally jumped at the sound. I don't have friends, for obvious reasons, and I never get deliveries because I don't buy anything aside from a little food and a lot of booze. Deciding it could only be a cold-caller of some description, I ignored it. The bell went again, along with a tap on the door. Not aggressive, just light and gentle, like a woman might knock... or a child.

Having just turned on the lamp, I couldn't exactly hide the fact I was home. I could take

Short Horror Stories Volume 3

a peek through the window, of course, but if I was seen then I'd need to open the door for sure. Deciding it couldn't do any harm, I pulled myself to my feet. I was swaying a little but I'd become a master at hiding my levels of inebriation, or so I thought.

I took a few steps to the window and pulled the curtain to one side, giving me a little crack to spy through. The small path which led to my front door was full of kids, no more than eight years old, all wrapped up against the cold. I counted twelve of them, with just one adult waiting on the pavement, their chaperone, I assumed. My addled brain first thought they must be out collecting Halloween sweets but then I remembered that holiday had passed already. *Do people give out sweets for Christmas?* I tried to remember.

Then, as one, all thirteen of my unwelcome visitors turned to face me. I felt as though I'd been slapped, such was the intensity of their glares even though mouths were smiling. I impulsively took a step back and lost my footing, causing an almighty clang as cans and bottles fell around me. *How long will they wait out there?* I felt... odd. I crawled on hands and knees to the window and took another peek, only to find they had gone.

Being the way I am, it's hard to rationalise many of my thoughts. It takes time to process my reactions to things. I sat, whiskey bottle in hand, beneath the window frame in my living room / bedroom for more than an

P.J. Blakey-Novis

hour. Processing. Trying to understand why I had felt so afraid of what must have been a group of fucking carol singers. Yeah, they're bloody annoying, but scary? Hardly. Eventually the anxiety and paranoia that fill me most of my waking hours returned to their normal, manageable level and I was able to sleep. A terrifying sleep that I could not recall details of as soon as my eyes opened.

December 21st, I felt on edge. Nothing particularly unusual about that but it was as though I'd forgotten something important, like an appointment. I couldn't place the reason for the feeling and I couldn't see anything that needed to be done, so I turned on the TV and opened a beer. My mind kept wandering to the idea of getting clean and this felt different. Almost as if I could actually do it. Naturally, I was drinking a beer early morning and I was under no illusions that I'd actually stop before passing out in around twelve hours' time. But something nagged at me, telling me to set a date, plan it properly, find a rehab clinic even.

10 days until New Year, I remember thinking. *If I can't drink myself to death by then, I'll get some fucking help.*

At 5.45pm the doorbell rang. My heart raced with a feeling that I'd been caught somewhere that I shouldn't be. I knew who was there before I even looked, but look I did. I moved the curtain a little to see twelve kids on my path and one adult, a chubby woman in her early twenties, waiting on the

Short Horror Stories Volume 3

pavement. Only this time, they were already looking in my direction. I nodded at them resignedly and made my way to the hall where I keep a dish of change. I scooped up a handful which was probably worth less than £3 and swung open the front door. With a forced smile on my face, I figured my best option was to indulge a few renditions of *Jingle Bells* and *We Wish You a Merry Christmas*, stick a handful of coins in whatever charity's tin they were collecting for, and enjoy the rest of the week in peace.

"Hello," I said, hoping I managed to get out a single word coherently.

"We want to sing you a song," a girl at the front said. She wore thick glasses, a hat and scarf, and a ridiculous 'ugly sweater' with a tractor on it. I couldn't exactly refuse her, right to her face, so I nodded and leaned against the hallway wall.

The darkness was thick when I awoke, forehead throbbing from a bump, wrist sore as though I'd fallen on it. I was in the hall, face pushed up against the skirting board. I hadn't vomited, so that was appreciated, but the smell of urine was unmistakable. *What the fuck had happened?* I don't tend to black out. I remember the carol singers, tractor-sweater girl was about to sing something, then... nothing. Had I passed out from the booze and they just left? The front door was closed, to my relief, so perhaps the chubby woman had seen I was simply hammered and left me to it. Not very Christian at Christmas

P.J. Blakey-Novis

time but who am I to judge? I felt groggy, muddled, so I stumbled along to the bathroom, emptied the potent contents of my bladder, and fell into a snoring heap on the airbed.

The clock read almost midday before I stirred. My head hurt, I felt like shit (more so than usual), and I dragged myself up with the intention of taking a shower. I couldn't remember the last time I'd had one and I was desperate to wash this headache away at the very least. I passed my filthy kitchen on the way to the bathroom and paused, eyes fixed on the fridge. *Beer?* The fact that I had paused to question it rather than grabbed a can on autopilot could be perceived as some kind of change. Instead of touching the fridge, I clicked on the kettle and scraped a spoonful of instant coffee into the least gross mug I could find on the worktop. I made a cupful, thick and black, and took it to the bathroom. I stripped, ran the shower, all the while staring into the cracked mirror on the wall. *What the fuck has happened to you?*

I took a few slurps of coffee and stood under the stream of almost scoldingly hot water. It stung in a good way. I felt something coming over me, a change, an awakening... a clarity. *Oh my God!* The nagging that had plagued me yesterday came to the forefront of my mind and hit me with a dizziness. *December 21st. It's been a whole year since... Since what?*

This day was different, I could feel it. As

213

Short Horror Stories Volume 3

though I'd reached the end of a year's sentence of complete misery, for the crime of being a drunken piece of shit. I stood on the bathroom tiles, wet and naked, finishing my coffee. Then, without bothering to dress, I searched the kitchen cupboards for black bags. *Time to sort this shit out,* I decided. Nothing was worth anything, so I took the quick way of cleaning and threw anything dirty in the bag, including plates and mugs, to join the empty cans, bottles, and ready-meal packages.

I threw away six fucking bin bags just from two rooms, heaping them at the end of my path and feeling something that could only have been shame or embarrassment. *Fuck,* I thought. *I've been a right fool.* I couldn't remember the last time I'd been outside the house but at that moment, under the crisp winter sun, it felt marvellous. It was time to venture further, so I grabbed my wallet and headed to the local convenience store for some cleaning supplies. I was on a mission and filled with something unfamiliar, something like... hope?

I took the long way home, marvelling at the fact it was almost 5.30pm and I'd only had coffee so far. I had no doubts I'd be grabbing a beer when I got home but it felt like one hell of an achievement, nevertheless. I'd showered, I'd tidied, I'd actually gone *outside*! And then my stomach dropped as I turned the corner to my street. I contemplated just walking past them, more out of

214

P.J. Blakey-Novis

embarrassment about last night than anything else. But I couldn't. The woman waiting on the pavement must have sensed me approaching as her head snapped in my direction. The kids all turned to look at me too, but slowly, almost perfectly in sync with each other. I was only a few feet from the end of my path at this point and I realised the six black bags had vanished. *Weird,* I thought, looking about. I could see no one else... the street was empty in both directions, houses blinked with festive lighting yet somehow looked discarded by the living.

"We want to sing you a song," I heard tractor-girl's voice, identical to the previous night. I felt exposed outside, but twelve kids on my tiny path were too many to squeeze past without touching them. I paused, awkwardly looking at the ever-silent adult.

"We want to sing you a song." A different voice this time, a boy. I couldn't tell who had spoken but I mumbled something about needing to get into the house to get some change for them, and then they could sing. The group parted a little, not offering to move away from my door but just about letting me through. I slipped my key into the lock, turned it, felt the door begin to move.

"WE WANT TO SING YOU A SONG!" Another voice, female but not tractor-girl's. The adult? Hard to tell. But this wasn't a sweet question, this came with a barrage of anger. This came from a place of hatred and vengeance. Within seconds I was in my

Short Horror Stories Volume 3

hallway, front door firmly shut, covering my ears as tiny hands knocked and knocked until my vision swam and I lost consciousness once again.

I didn't drink yesterday, of that I was certain. I rarely forgot what I'd done anyway, and I distinctly remembered showering, tidying, going out, and... those fucking carol singers. So how did I end up on the hallway floor if I was sober? I reached for the light switch, stepped into the living room. Just after 2am. Shit everywhere. Well, by 'shit' I mean all the empty cans and chip wrappers that I could swear I'd thrown away yesterday. Frowning, I checked the kitchen. Same shit, different room. Had I really dreamt about cleaning? What a fucking weirdo.

The next point of confusion came when it was no longer clear what day it was. December 21st, I could remember. Felt weird, singers came, woke up in hall. Woke up... on the 22nd. But if that day was a dream, is it just the start of the 22nd now? Or the 23rd... but that would make the dream real and would mean someone had brought all my rubbish back inside. I was giving myself a headache thinking about this stuff so I opened a beer. I grabbed a bin bag, went to the living room, and started to fill it again. Ideally, I was looking for my phone that I vaguely recall throwing somewhere after a shitty text from Jenny. The phone would have the date, and then maybe I'd know what was happening.

216

P.J. Blakey-Novis

Eventually I found it, sticky and dusty, but it lit up once the charger was connected. Turned it on. Ignored all the spam messages which came through. Focused on the home screen. 2.34am. Monday, December 21st. *Fuck.*

Nothing made sense, but nothing had for a long time. Had I gone insane? Questions came with such force my head began to pound, like a physical manifestation of a question I wouldn't like the answer to. But what was the question that *truly* mattered? It was there, digging away at my sanity, threatening to open some area of my mind I'd compartmentalised and bolted shut with a giant sign that said *This shit's too traumatic, keep it fucking closed.*

How certain was I that the doorbell first rang on the 20th? Not very. I'd based the date on the calendar... how stupid is that? The boxes are blank so how would I know what day it is? Only I *did* know. I was sure at the time. But if it's only now the 21st, it must have been the 18th when I didn't answer. Logic said that was the case, but I wasn't buying it. *What about the rubbish? Why did I black out? What's so special about the 21st?*

I was getting nowhere so I went out. I don't remember the last time I'd gone outside in the middle of the night. It felt weird. A nervous energy had settled over me, as though the streets weren't entirely safe but there was some excitement in that fact.

I couldn't make sense of anything and

217

Short Horror Stories Volume 3

knew I never would unless I sobered up, and for good. But all that rattled around in my head was the date, December 21st... December 21st... December 21st. Why was it so damned important?

I must have walked for a few hours because the first hints of pale blue and faint orange were beginning to stream through the grey clouds. I'd only had the one beer since waking so there was no danger of any alcohol-related hallucinations or other weirdness. Which made the sight of twelve kids filling my pathway all the more surprising.

I was still at least ten houses away from my own, the streets silent in the early morning. Multi-coloured lights flickered from decorated trees in windows, wreaths hung on doors, the occasional inflatable Santa or snowman flopped lazily near the pavement. All was as it should be at this time of year, everything was *natural*.

Except my own visitors. They were far from explainable, the complete opposite of the expected. Something sinister, malevolent... vengeful.

I walked past them, just to see what would happen. They stared at my door, oblivious to my passing, until their adult chaperone must have clocked me. Then all eyes moved as one but they did not leave my path. I crossed the road and watched for a bit. They stared at me as I returned their gaze. I'd be lying if I said I wasn't afraid but I needed to know what they

P.J. Blakey-Novis

were doing there. And my first mission was to find out if anyone else could see them.

6.40am. We stood on the cold street, watching each other.

6.55am. I wandered down the road to the convenience store I knew opens at 7am. I grabbed a bottle of water, a chocolate bar and a newspaper.

7.05am. I'm back in the spot opposite my house. *They* are still there. Only now they are smiling. I give an involuntary shudder, telling myself I'm just cold and not afraid. Telling myself yet another lie.

7.30am. Still no sign of another soul which, quite frankly, is weird. No lights have come on in any windows, nobody walking a dog. Only person I'd seen that I was certain actually existed was the guy running the shop but he's not going to close up and come tell me if I'm seeing things.

7.45am. *Fuck this,* I decided. *It's my house and I need a nap.* I knew I'd not be able to sleep but my brain was trying to be assertive over my body, I guess. Just as before, the kids parted just enough to let me pass. I stuck the key in, opened the door. Was about to kick it closed behind me to avoid any further eye contact when I paused. I turned, somehow drawn to tractor-girl. She seemed to be a leader of sorts. "What do you want?" I asked.

"We want to sing you a song," she said, her head tilting to her right. A split-second later and all other heads tilted in an exact replica.

Short Horror Stories Volume 3

"We want to sing you a song," thirteen voices screeched in unison. I kicked the door closed and backed away from it, darkness swirled in front of my eyes, and I awoke once again in my hallway, forehead throbbing from another (or was it the same?) bump.

Same thing, almost. Like an imitation Groundhog Day... similar but not identical, as though someone were trying to trick me. Whatever was happening was beyond my comprehension and this only served to make me angry. Harassed by carol singers, confused and bumped about, nursing an eternal hangover, tired... everything pissed me off. But the most frustrating thing was the secret that still somehow eluded me. I knew it would hold the answers and it all came down to just one question. What was so fucking special about December 21st?

The booze wasn't bringing forth any answers and neither was staying hidden in my house. Hiding from a bunch of screechy kids? What a pussy. Only... they're not *just* a bunch of screechy kids, are they? And they won't be leaving me alone any time soon, of that I was certain.

My clock said a little after eleven in the morning. After a piss and a swish of mouthwash, I yanked the front door open. Still there, the little fuckers. I started to shove my way through them but they seemed less inclined to make space this time. Angrier.

"What do you want?" I asked, still taking

steps towards the end of my path and the perceived safety of the street.

"We want to sing you a song," a boy next to me said. His eyes fixed on mine and he looked nothing but sad. I kept moving forward. Reaching the pavement, I faced the woman who always accompanied this rabble yet never seemed to have any control.

"I think you should take them somewhere else now," I told her. "I'm going out for a bit and you lot better not be here when I get back or I'll have the coppers move you on."

No response, just an empty stare. Frustrated, I took off down the street and towards the small town centre. Thank God it had just passed pub opening time.

Small town, shit pubs, but cheap and quiet. Both of these factors were essential in my current situation. The date was still bugging me, so I asked the barmaid to tell me what day, month, and year it was as she poured me a pint of Harvey's. She looked at me as though I thought I was being hilarious and was about to claim to be a time-traveller.

"December 21st, 2023. Why?"

"Something about the date is bugging me. Feels familiar."

"Your wedding anniversary?" she suggested, as though it were the most obvious thing in the world. "Or a kid's birthday?"

I shook my head. "Something bigger."

"Where were you this time last year?"

Partial realisation began to hit as the bar

Short Horror Stories Volume 3

swirled. The hand holding the pint shook, causing it to spill a little on the sticky countertop. A cold gust whipped around the room, flapping strings of tinsel and causing the garish baubles on the tree to clang about.

I needed to sit and fumbled for the stool to my right, the barmaid looking concerned and reaching for my arm but I could barely hear her. Only one sound rang through my mind at that moment and reluctantly I turned to face that hideous fucking tractor jumper. *We want to sing you a song. We want to sing you a song. We want to sing...*

I collapsed to the floor, memories flooding back in agonising bursts. How could I have forgotten? Sure, I didn't recall the exact date, but I knew where I was this time last year, for the whole week. In a coma.

We want to sing you a song.

And what had led to an alcoholic waste of space such as myself to be in a coma? Why, a traffic incident of course.

We want to sing you a song.

I'm sure you can guess whose fault the accident was. Trying to open another bottle and took both hands off the steering wheel for a second or two. Long enough to lose control. To cross the white lines. To make the bus driver swerve. I hit a wall, the car went flying, I woke up eight days later.

We want to sing you a song.

The bus driver made it. So did more than half the kids, if you're inclined to look on the positive side of things. One teaching assistant

P.J. Blakey-Novis

and twelve little kiddies didn't make it though. Because of me. And now they just want to sing me a fucking song?!

"So sing it already!" I screamed, dropping to my knees in front of tractor girl. I could sense the barmaid to my left, some other movement behind me. I didn't know if anyone else could see what I saw but it didn't matter, not anymore. I needed resolution, forgiveness, some way to move forward.

The kids all stared as one, smiled suddenly, and opened their mouths in unison. I wondered if I was really seeing thirteen spirits or if it was something more malevolent taking on this guise. I would never know.

"Forgive me?" I asked.

"Never," they whispered as one. Then they began to sing. A hauntingly beautiful melody which sounded both festive and ancient, like something you'd hear in a grand cathedral on Christmas Day. I felt a tear run down my cheek as my sight left me and I fell forward, my face against the rough, stinking carpet of the pub. The tune continued and I felt my body grow weaker. How could I refuse them? I didn't want to die, but then what reason did I have to live? As I faded out, I could only hope eternity would give me some chance at redemption.

Short Horror Stories Volume 3

Sister Mary

I was nineteen when my parents died, a drunk driver jumping a red light and ploughing into the side of their VW. That was also the time at which I discovered Martha and Noah weren't my real parents. Apparently, I was never supposed to know but Jessica (whom I'd thought was my blood-sister) decided she'd tell me when it came to going through the will. It wasn't a caring, I-thought-you-should-know kind of revelation; it was more along the lines of *She's not blood so she shouldn't get anything.*

Numb is the only way I can describe the weeks that followed. The shock of their death, followed by the news of my adoption as a baby, added to by my only 'sister' turning against me, all took its toll. It was the first time in my life I'd felt truly alone. However, with Jessica being two years younger than me, I was appointed her legal guardian, at least until she turned eighteen. We inherited the family home, a small amount in savings, and a life insurance settlement. Much to Jessica's disapproval, this was split down the middle, with her unable to access her share until her next birthday.

The months that came after were filled with fights over money, fights about the chores around the house, and as much as I attempted to act like Jessica's guardian, she rebelled against me. She'd stay out all night without checking in and she'd return home barely able to walk from the alcohol she'd consumed. I loved Jessica, I still do, and after a few months of stress I decided to take a step back. She was grieving, and lost, and she needed to get it out of her system.

Once I had *gotten off her back*, as she had put it, the hostility began to dissipate. She even invited me to a few parties. Our new routine was a far cry from how things had been when our parents were alive, but we were beginning to manage. We even talked about the future.

"When I'm eighteen," Jessica began, tentatively, "I want to get my own place."

I paused, having been expecting this. "Okay," I said.

"I think we should sell the house, with a fifty-fifty split, of course. Then we can get our own places," she explained. I must have looked upset by this, and perhaps I was, because she went on. "It's not that I don't want to live with you, Cassie, I just thought, as we'd both be adults..." Jessica looked at the ground.

"You're right," I said, trying to force a smile. "It's the normal thing to do. I guess I just don't feel ready to be on my own."

"Sorry," Jessica mumbled. "It won't be until my birthday, so there are a few months yet. And it could take a while for the house to sell. Plus, we can still see each other all the time – I don't plan to move far away." I

Short Horror Stories Volume 3

nodded but said nothing. The creeping dread of being alone was beginning to set in again, its dark fingers working their way around my throat. I shivered.

"There's something else," Jessica said. This time she looked at me, despite her obvious discomfort. The first thought that came to mind was that she was pregnant, and maybe that would have been less concerning. "I found this."

I reached across to take the brown envelope which she was offering me. The outside was blank, and I had absolutely no idea what to expect. Jessica stayed silent as I tore it open and pulled the sheets of paper out. I scanned the first page before looking up. "So?" I asked. "You already told me I was adopted." I'd read the first page and that only confirmed what I already knew. If Jessica hadn't told me then it would have been a huge shock, of course, but this wasn't anything new.

"Read the second page," she said.

I scanned through the second and third pages, reaching the end of the file. "What about it?" I asked, still not wanting to think about Noah and Martha not being my biological parents. They had raised me, and I loved them for it, that was all that mattered.

"Your birth mother's name is on there," Jessica stated, as if I hadn't noticed.

"Yeah," I muttered. "I saw."

"So, we should find her!" Jessica declared, a little too enthusiastically.

P.J. Blakey-Novis

"If she didn't want me then, why would she want anything to do with me now?" I asked. "And why would I want anything to do with her? For all we know she's dead too, or a junkie. I can't see anything good can come of this." I stood up, keen to change the subject.

"She may well be a terrible person," Jessica said. "But if you don't find out for yourself then you'll always wonder. While we have this time still together, I can help."

I knew she wouldn't drop it and, as much as my mind screamed at me to let this one go, I relented. "Okay, Miss Marple," I began, attempting to lighten the mood, "I'll grab some wine and you get your laptop. We'll see what we can find out online, but I have no intention in making contact with this woman, even if we do find out where she is. Deal?" Jessica nodded enthusiastically, leaping from the sofa and disappearing to her bedroom to retrieve her laptop. Regardless of the situation, it was nice to be able to do something with Jessica.

I'd never had much interest in social media so left Jessica to it as I sipped my wine. She informed me that Facebook is what the older people use so she started there. Typing in the name *Mary McBride*, Jessica showed me a list of six matches. Five of them looked to be around my age and one was of a skin tone too dark to be my parent. "Weird," she muttered.

"Not really," I replied. "Did you really think it'd be that easy? Not everyone is on

227

Short Horror Stories Volume 3

Facebook, and certainly not if she's dead, or some junkie prostitute."

"Fine," Jessica said, bringing up the search engine's homepage and typing the name and geographical area into it. I'd reached across to refill my wine glass when I heard my sister mutter *Shit!*

"What?" I asked, scanning the results on the screen before us. *Mary McBride, previously a nun in the Order of Damascus, has been charged with the murder of three colleagues.* "That can't be her," I said, refusing to believe it.

"That was April 2000," Jessica said. "Six months before you were born."

"Seriously?" I said, once again standing up. "You actually think this killer nun is my mum? That's ridiculous!"

"I mean, it's insane," Jessica said, half-grinning, "but it explains why she had to give you up."

"I can't believe you think this is funny!" I said.

"You're a prison baby!" Jessica replied, now beginning to laugh. "I'm sorry, but that is pretty funny."

"Keep searching," I said, allowing a smile. "There must be more options than just the nun. And you really think a nun would be pregnant? Isn't that completely against what they stand for?"

Jessica looked at me as if I were a moron. "You think nun-mum would turn down sex for religious reasons but was okay with

P.J. Blakey-Novis

butchering three other nuns?"

"Fine," I said, "but don't call her nun-mum. It's weird."

We spent another hour trawling through the matches for my birth mother's name but came up with nothing. The only possibilities were Mary the murdering nun, or someone who had left no online trail, and Jessica insisted the latter was impossible.

"Okay, so maybe, just maybe, this Mary is my mother. What do you suggest we do?" I asked. After finishing the first bottle of wine and having made a dent in a second, I was feeling much bolder than I had to begin with. I'd managed to block out any genuine emotions and was treating this like a fantasy.

"To be honest," Jessica said, "if she's locked up then maybe that's for the best. It means you could visit her without it getting weird. She wouldn't need to know where you live, she wouldn't be able to see you without you agreeing to it."

"Visit her?" I asked, genuinely surprised. "In a prison?"

"Not exactly," Jessica replied, pointing to her laptop screen.

The website for *Mayfield Psychiatric Hospital* was displayed. I suddenly felt myself sober up as reality hit. The place wasn't too far away, and it was feeling more and more likely that Mary was truly my birth mother. A shiver ran through me – something felt wrong, but I put it down to nerves. The emotions I had tried to bury came flooding to

Short Horror Stories Volume 3

the surface and I burst into tears, catching Jessica off-guard. She had been right, I needed to know. I needed to meet Mary.

Despite the wine, I did not sleep soundly that night. Whatever had filled my dreams is hard to describe, appearing more in colour than shape, violent flashes of red and black. Bizarre symbols and unsettling images blurred in my mind against the soundtrack of a thousand screaming voices. I awoke, drenched in sweat, my hands trembling.

Jessica was already at the coffee machine by the time I'd got downstairs and she helpfully pointed out how terrible I looked. She passed me a strong black coffee and a buttered croissant, grinning like she had something important to say.

"What?" I asked, not in the mood for games. "I didn't sleep well, and I have a banging headache."

Jessica pulled some painkillers from the kitchen drawer and fetched me a glass of water. "Take these, finish your coffee, and get in the shower. You can't go anywhere looking like that."

"I'm not going anywhere," I said, having assumed I was about to be dragged on yet another shopping trip.

"We have an appointment," Jessica said. "And if you show up to the nut-house looking like that they will try to keep you there!"

I stared at her, a handful of croissant an inch from my mouth. "What have you done?" I asked.

P.J. Blakey-Novis

"We're off to see nun-mum at eleven," she declared. "And don't even try to get out of it. I called the place this morning and made the arrangements." I fought back tears, emotions pulling me in all directions. Most of me wanted to go back to bed, sleep off my hangover, forget about Mary. But there was that nagging part that knew Jessica was right, and if I didn't go now then I may never do so.

"Urgh, fine!" I told her. "I'll go, but we go in together and just to find out if she is who we think she is. Then we leave, possibly forever." Jessica held out her pinky finger and we shook on it.

The life insurance money we had inherited may not have been a huge amount, but to us, at that age, it felt like an endless supply of cash. This had made us lazy and, with neither of us able to drive, we took an expensive cab ride to the *Mayfield Psychiatric Hospital*, rather than the cheaper bus option. The first thing that struck me as we exited the taxi was how nice the place was. It could easily have been mistaken for a luxury spa hotel.

Jessica took the lead, pressing the entry buzzer at the main gates. I stayed a few steps behind, clasping my hands together to conceal the trembling. I felt nauseous, nerves getting the better of me, as the twin gates swung open with a creak. As we made our way along the drive to the main entrance, the crunching of gravel beneath our feet was the

Short Horror Stories Volume 3

only sound we could hear. The main door swung open as we approached it, a vicar waiting to greet us.

"You must be Cassie," the man said, looking at Jessica.

"Nope," she answered, nodding her head towards me.

"Hi," I mumbled, extending my hand. The vicar, who introduced himself as Father Benjamin, took my hand in his sweaty one and shook it.

"You're here to see Mary?"

"Yes," Jessica interjected before I could speak. "Was it you I spoke to on the phone?"

"It was," Father Benjamin confirmed, leading us into the lobby. The place was spotless, as one would expect from a hospital, but was eerily silent. I was uncomfortable, not only due to the weight of the situation, but there was something else bothering me – I just couldn't put my finger on it.

"Sorry," I said, trying to choose my words carefully. "Before we see Mary, could I speak to one of the doctors? I'd like to find out a bit more about how she is doing."

"My dear child," Father Benjamin began, his words coming out in a patronising tone, "we are not a hospital in the traditional sense. We don't employ doctors of medicine. This is a church-run facility and we like to call ourselves doctors of the soul." He gave a little chuckle at this point.

"But if she has psychiatric difficulties," I

232

P.J. Blakey-Novis

pressed, "then surely that needs to be attended to by a medical professional."

"Are you suggesting that your head doctors know more than Almighty God?" the vicar asked me, a flash of anger in his eyes. I felt Jessica nudge me and I let it drop.

"I'm sure that's not what Cassie meant," she said, smiling sweetly. "Perhaps you would be able to give us a bit of background about Mary? You seem to be in charge here." *Creep,* I thought, but it was working. Father Benjamin turned his focus to Jessica and directed us to one of the seats in the lobby.

"Mary has been under our supervision for almost twenty years," he began. "You said on the telephone that you'd seen the newspaper articles? An unfortunate business."

"She killed three people?" Jessica asked, fishing for the vicar's opinion on the matter. I stayed quiet, beginning to feel as though this were a waste of time.

"No, *she* did not," Father Benjamin said, much to both mine and Jessica's surprise. "The entity that lives within her killed three people." *Here we go,* I thought, resisting the urge to walk out. Jessica clearly had more patience than I did.

"Entity?" she pressed.

"Do you have any religious beliefs?" Father Benjamin asked, his eyes still only on Jessica.

"Not really," she admitted. He glanced at me briefly as I shook my head.

"Mary McBride was in the service of the

Short Horror Stories Volume 3

church from the age of seventeen. She was a devout and wholesome woman, until that *thing* got a hold of her." He almost spat the words. "We still don't know how it happened for sure, but it seems to stem from a missionary trip she went on in late 1999, to some rather heathen villages in Africa. You know the sort of places, full of witchdoctors and cannibals. No place for honest, God-fearing people." The man's prejudices were grating on me, but I held my tongue.

"Some of the other sisters caught her in an unwholesome act with the gardener in the January of 2000. I won't go into detail." *My father!* I realised. "Sister Mary was reprimanded of course and prayed for forgiveness, but a bastard child had already taken root inside her." Father Benjamin sounded disgusted by the tale he was relaying and oblivious to calling me a *bastard child* right to my face.

"Naturally, the church wanted to keep the situation quiet and transferred the gardener to another district with a generous donation 'for his troubles'. The intention was to keep Sister Mary confined to her room until the child came, and then her offspring would be placed in adoptive care. We did not know that she was no longer in control until that night."

"What makes you think she wasn't in control?" Jessica asked. "Could she not simply have wanted to leave? If she was being held against her will, perhaps she tried to escape, and things escalated?"

234

P.J. Blakey-Novis

"Escape?" Father Benjamin looked incredulous. "It was a convent, not a prison! Sister Mary was there of her own free will. Even if she had decided to leave her post in the church, which is highly doubtful, she would not murder three of her close friends in such a gruesome manner! Something came back from those Godless villages with her, and that is why she is here."

"Can I use the toilet before we see her?" I interrupted, looking at Jessica and hoping she would take the hint.

"Good idea," Jessica stated, standing before the vicar could speak. "Which way?" Father Benjamin pointed along the hallway and muttered that the door is to the right. We didn't speak until we were safely inside.

"He's fucking nuts," Jessica said, trying to control a fit of giggles.

"Yep," I agreed, "But I'm worried, Jess."

"About what? That your mum's possessed?" She let out a laugh at this point.

"No, that she may need actual medical care, not this religious nonsense. No wonder she's still in here, if all the help she gets is prayers."

"So, get her out," Jessica said flatly. "You must be her next-of-kin. Insist on a proper doctor seeing her." I nodded my head, beginning to feel as though I needed to help this woman I had never met.

"Ready?" Jessica asked, about to open the door back to the hallway.

"I'll be out in a minute," I said, nodding

Short Horror Stories Volume 3

towards the cubicle. I did my business and began washing my hands when the lights went out. It was only for a fraction of a second, but it was enough to startle me. I held my hands under the dryer, its sound filling the small room, when the lights went out for a second time. The perfect darkness of the room flickered from black to red, reminding me of my dream the previous night. When the lights came back on, Jessica was standing in front of me, her foot holding the door open.

"What's wrong?" she asked, looking more confused than concerned.

"Sorry," I mumbled again, "The lights went out and it made me jump."

"The lights haven't done anything; I've been stood here the whole time. Anyway, the creepy vicar is ready to take us down now," she said, far too loudly. I glanced around the bathroom, confused and on-edge.

"Okay," I told her, following behind.

The luxurious appearance of the place was entirely for the benefit of those visitors who had no need to travel beyond the ground floor. From the outside we could see there were two floors above ground and had assumed that Mary was in one of those rooms. When Father Benjamin ushered us into a lift and pressed the -2 button, I felt a flutter of panic. Basements were never good. The lift shuddered to life, Jessica and the vicar chatting about the history of the building, seemingly oblivious to the lights

236

P.J. Blakey-Novis

flickering on and off, the darkness switching from red to black. I could still see them, silhouetted in the angry colours, but it was as if they had forgotten about me. I tried to speak but nothing came out. As suddenly as the lights had gone out, they were back on and the door slid open.

Two floors below ground, the 'ward', as Father Benjamin had called it, was in need of maintenance. It may well have been a ward at some point, but as I made my way along it all I could see were empty rooms. There was no doubt that something was very wrong, and I began to wonder if Mary was even down here. Jessica and I had allowed ourselves to be led underground by a man who made me feel uncomfortable – there was no telling what he had planned for us. I was about to turn back when the man spoke.

"Here we are," he stated, coming to a stop outside a thick, metal door. "Now, as I've tried to explain, there isn't much of Mary left in there. She's restrained but I'd recommend making the visit short."

"In case we get possessed?" Jessica asked, her sarcasm fully on display.

"This is no joking matter," Father Benjamin replied.

"I just don't understand," Jessica continued. "If you honestly believe in what you are saying, why let us see her?"

"If Cassie is her daughter, then she has a right to visit," he said with a shrug, as though it were the most obvious thing.

237

Short Horror Stories Volume 3

Pulling a ring of keys from his pocket, Father Benjamin unlocked the door and called into the room. It was in complete darkness and I waited for him to switch on a light, but he did not. "Sister Mary, you have a visitor." He did not step over the threshold to the room.

"Are you going to turn the light on then?" Jessica asked, becoming impatient. Everything about this felt off now, but if Jess had picked up on it then she kept it to herself.

"Sometimes she doesn't like the light," Father Benjamin said.

"Well, we're going to need a light on before you get two young girls to walk into a room in your basement." Father Benjamin looked shocked at the insinuation, but I felt relieved that Jessica and I were thinking the same thing. We watched as the vicar reached into the room, his hands fumbling along the wall to the right. I heard a click before the darkness of the room evaporated and I let out a gasp.

Sister Mary, the woman who may be my mother, was crouched in the corner of the room. Her ankles were shackled together with a chain that was fixed to the wall. She was pale and malnourished; she looked close to death. My first desire was to scream at that bastard vicar for treating her this way, my second thought was to run to the woman and hold her. I did neither. Jessica took hold of my hand, squeezing it hard. I could sense her fear. We took a couple of steps inside the

P.J. Blakey-Novis

room, under the watchful gaze of Sister Mary. I screamed as the door closed behind us, the lock clicking into place.

Jessica began banging on the metal of the door, the thuds reverberating around the cell, for that's what it truly was. No sound came from the other side. I looked at Mary, fixed to the spot, staring at us. No emotion registered on her face but her eyes were set on me so I knew she could tell we were there.

"Sister Mary?" I said quietly, meeting her gaze. "I'm Cassie." Jessica turned away from the door and joined me in staring at the shell of this woman.

"I'm scared," she whispered. I nodded, trying to keep my own fear at bay. Now that we were here, I needed to know if this woman was my mother.

"Sister Mary, can I come closer?" I asked, taking a step towards her.

The nun's head turned to the side, her expression now inquisitive. We watched her mouth open just a little, enough to let out a low, guttural moan. "Not if you want to live!" the voice said, much deeper than it should have been.

Jessica was back at the door, hammering on it as tears flowed freely. I was still unconvinced by Father Benjamin's diagnosis, despite what I could see before me. My mind whirred with possible explanations – schizophrenia being at the forefront, alongside Munchausen by Proxy. If she had been told she was possessed by a demon for

239

Short Horror Stories Volume 3

the last twenty years, kept locked in this cell and treated like a monster, surely that would manifest itself in some way. I decided to take a different approach.

"Mum?" I asked, holding my breath as I waited on a reply. Something flickered in Mary's eyes, a hint of recognition, perhaps. Her head tilted to the other side as her eyes stayed fixed on mine. "I think you're my mother," I continued, braving a step forward. "You had a relationship, of sorts, with the gardener? I'm sorry, I don't know his name."

Sister Mary's mouth turned up into a smile, impossibly large, rotten teeth on display. "I rode his cock in the gardens, much to the dismay of my sisters," she said, her voice still inhumanly deep. "Those little sluts looked at me with disgust, but I could smell them dampen as they watched."

I didn't know what to say, everything I was seeing fitted with what Father Benjamin had said, but that was impossible, surely? Jessica seemed to have not heard the words coming from this woman and kept hammering on the door.

"The gardener put you inside me for a reason," Sister Mary continued, her voice now feminine and almost kind-sounding.

"So, you *are* my mother?" I asked, my back now against the wall.

"Yes, child. And I need you to get me out of this place. That man, that so-called vicar, is a monster. He has kept me locked away in here for so long."

240

P.J. Blakey-Novis

"Don't listen to her," Jessica yelled at me. "He was right, that *thing* is a monster!"

The room turned to darkness, thick black destroying my vision. The flickers of violent colour from my nightmare reappeared, changing the room from black to red and back again. It was as if I was in a nightclub under a blood-red strobe light. I could see staggered movement, like a jumpy animation. I watched as Sister Mary's mouth opened impossibly wide, releasing something black into the air. The smell that accompanied it made me gag, like rotten eggs and spoiled chicken. The black form moved away from Sister Mary, seeming to cause her to crumple to the floor, before surrounding Jessica. I felt stuck in place, as though the air had become impenetrably thick. I watched in horror as Jessica smashed her own face into the metal door, over and again. I could make out the dark trails of blood dripping onto the floor from her shattered nose. With one final thrust, Jessica hit her forehead against the metal with a crack and dropped. The black mass returned to Sister Mary, the lights came back on, and I finally screamed.

Father Benjamin returned to the cell the following day, bringing with him two other priests armed with tasers. They shackled me in the same way as Sister Mary, before dragging my sister's lifeless body from the room. I tried to plead with them, to no avail.

"I needed to know if you really were that

Short Horror Stories Volume 3

child," Father Benjamin explained, not a hint of regret in his voice. "Unfortunately for you, it seems as though you are."

"You can't just keep me here!" I said, now terrified that I'd be left to rot in this basement for the rest of my life.

"I'm afraid I can," he replied. "You were created because of the entity inside of Sister Mary. You are unclean and must remain here. It is safest for both you and the rest of humanity. We can't very well have demons roaming around free, can we?"

"So do a fucking exorcism!" I shouted.

"Too expensive," he replied, shrugging once more. "We'd have to fly a professional in from Rome. At least this way we can contain the demon here." I watched Father Benjamin leave the room and heard the click of the lock. This was to be my life now, trapped in this dingy cell with a mother I've never known, and a creature I don't want to know.

"Mum?" I asked, looking at Sister Mary. "What are we going to do?"

"We're going to get out of here, my child," came my mother's deep, otherworldly voice. "And we're going to watch this place burn." I smiled, knowing that she was telling the truth.

242

P.J. Blakey-Novis

Cassie and the Demon

With a lack of natural light, there had been no way to discern between day and night. For the first few days since arriving at the *Mayfield Psychiatric Hospital* I'd managed to keep the time fairly straight in my head but now I had no idea how long we had been there for. My best guess would be around a month, but I could be wrong.

I'd visited with my sister (stepsister, in fact, as I'd recently discovered), on a mission to locate my birth mother. Our trawling of the Internet had led us to this God-forsaken institute, run by Father Benjamin, in the hope of meeting with Sister Mary. We'd found her, what was left of her, but she was not in a good way.

I'd never put much thought into religion and I still went over the events of that day in my mind. We'd arrived and been greeted by Father Benjamin. He had relayed his strong belief that my mother, Sister Mary, was being possessed by some entity that had latched itself on to her on a missionary trip to Africa before I was born. This, according to Father Benjamin, is what had caused her to have sex with the gardener at the convent, my father.

As I said, my stepsister, Jessica, came with me on that fateful day. She's no longer with us – whatever demon has taken up residence

243

Short Horror Stories Volume 3

inside Sister Mary took Jessica's life and Father Benjamin, of this I have no doubt, disposed of the body in secret. In my mind, he is as much of a monster as the demon itself.

The room I now share with my mother, and the thing that has taken root within her, is more of a cell. There are no windows. The only contact with anyone outside of the room is a twice-daily visit with just enough food to keep us alive. There is only one cot bed, so I usually sleep on the cold floor. We spent the first few days, the ones that I could keep track of, getting to know one another. To begin with I was terrified, the voice coming from Sister Mary alternating between feminine and monstrous, but I became accustomed to it.

Mary, for that is the only name I know to use, promised me that we'd get out of this place, but I knew it was not her voice which made that vow. I also had no doubt that Father Benjamin would keep me in that place for the rest of my life if he could, convinced as he was that I was now the Devil's own spawn. I also knew that, even if this demon left of its own accord, Father Benjamin would never believe it. Like it or not, I needed this monster to help us escape.

The demon and I spent hours in conversation once my fear had subsided. I was angry with it, of course, for the brutal slaying of Jessica, but this demon had a way with words. Had he been human, he would

P.J. Blakey-Novis

undoubtedly take the form of a smooth-talking man preying on women. When I had first stood up to him, really screamed in his/Mary's face, he'd been surprised. I think I even sensed that he was impressed. He reminded me that I would not exist if it weren't for him, which, unfortunately, I couldn't disagree with.

Even in the comparatively short time I spent in that cell (Sister Mary having had been there since before my birth), I could see her fading away and the demon's strength growing. It wouldn't be too much longer before she was entirely demon and I asked what would happen when Mary's body failed completely. Mary shrugged, or rather the demon shrugged Mary's body for her, and replied simply, "I move on to another." Being the only other person there I could see my fate.

"Can't you move on to one of the priests?" I asked. "Not wanting to point out the obvious, but if you did that you could release me and go on to possess whoever you like." A growl came from Mary.

"No priests," she said, her voice low and animalistic. "Too holy."

"Are they though?" I asked. "Is it their genuine beliefs that stop you, or just the crosses around their necks? Father Benjamin isn't a good person, that much is obvious." I watched Mary's head cock to the side as though in thought. Perhaps this demon wasn't as clever as he thought he was.

Short Horror Stories Volume 3

"Both," Mary growled.

"But you got into Mary," I went on, thinking aloud more than conversing with the creature, "and she was holy."

"I was invited," he said, through my mother's mouth. The look on my face must have shown that I did not believe that. "A witchdoctor summoned me a long time ago, I bounced from one villager to the next. Mary invited me in so that I'd leave the children of the village in safety. I'd not managed to infiltrate the church before, so I took the chance."

"Didn't work out too well for you," I said, before thinking about it.

"I wouldn't say that, the gardener was quite fun," Mary replied with a smirk.

"We need to get out of here," I said again, frustrated that I seemed to need this thing's help.

"I killed your sister, took control of your mother's body, and you tried to have me exorcised. Why would I trust you? I'm sure you'd like to see me gone."

"Even if you left, Father Benjamin would put it down to 'the Devil's tricks' and keep me here anyway. I only see two options..."

"Two?"

"I lure one of the priests in here, maybe snatch off his cross, and you take over his body or..."

"Or?"

"Or we exorcise you so they can see you've gone."

P.J. Blakey-Novis

"They didn't seem to go for that when you last suggested it." I knew I'd need to think of a plan for myself as this allegedly all-powerful demon seemed content to rot in this cell.

Bearing in mind that Father Benjamin and his gang of priests were happy to leave me in that room until my death, it wasn't easy to think of ways to get them to open the door. The demon was clear about his powers, especially his ability to create fire out of nothing. I toyed with the notion of burning the bed but doubted anyone would come to our rescue. With the lack of ventilation, we'd be dead in minutes from smoke inhalation.

I came up with a number of ideas, all of which were useless. All except one. Sister Mary had to die.

It wasn't an easy decision to make but I knew it was the right one. Aside from my own desperation to be free of that place, this was no life for the nun. A terrifying thought hit me – What if Father Benjamin doesn't allow me to leave, possession aside? Surely he is breaking some law by keeping me here or was he right that the church's power supersedes the laws of man? I decided it was a chance I had to take.

"If Mary's body dies, you'll come into mine?" I asked, wanting clarity. A grin spread across Mary's face, impossibly wide, which I took as a yes. "So, I'll make you a deal." Making deals with demons isn't something I

Short Horror Stories Volume 3

ever thought I'd be doing, and every rational thought told me it was a bad idea, but I did it anyway. "You allow Mary to die, peacefully, and you take my body. I don't believe that even Father Benjamin would leave a corpse, especially not a nun's corpse, to rot in here. That's when we make our move." It wasn't a flawless plan by any means, and I knew the demon would just take me when the time came, but it was the best I could come up with. I knew it was risky but felt as though I had no choice. "But," I went on, "when we are out of this place you leave me. I don't care where you go, but you get out."

"Sure," the voice said, my mother's dull eyes staring blankly in my direction. I didn't trust the demon, naturally, but again, no choice. I spent that evening holding on to my mother, feeling how frail she was, her bones rigid beneath my hands. When I awoke she was gone and, for a moment, I felt normal. Then I vomited. A torrent of thick black gunk sprayed from my throat and I knew I wasn't alone inside my head. I stood, pacing about the room, feeling like myself yet not, as though I was suddenly stronger, angrier. It was time to put the plan into action and I began hammering at the door.

For a while I thought they were going to simply ignore the banging but I was relentless, smashing my fists into the cold metal until the skin glowed red. Eventually, one of the priests who often delivered the food came to the door, shouting through it. I

248

P.J. Blakey-Novis

explained the situation, that Sister Mary had passed away, through a torrent of genuine tears. The priest scurried away, returning surprisingly quickly with Father Benjamin.

"Cassie," he called, "Father Davies told me about your mother's untimely death." *Untimely?* I thought. *He sounds like he's giving condolences at a fucking funeral, not to his prisoner.*

"Yes," I replied, the tears still falling. "I thought you'd need to know so that she can have a proper burial." Father Benjamin seemed to be mulling something over as there was a pause.

"And the entity?" he asked. I also paused, unsure what he would believe.

"Still within her or gone, perhaps. I honestly don't know."

"Or within you?" he said.

"I don't feel any different," I replied. "I'm not expecting you to just let me out, I just want Sister Mary's body removed and treated with respect. So that her soul can be at peace." I heard a sigh from beyond the door and knew he had relented. *Now's the time,* the voice in my head said. I/We stood in place as the bolts clicked to one side, the door opening just a crack. The priest Davies poked his head around the door, presumably to verify that Mary had indeed passed.

I lost control in the most literal way. I could see, hear, and feel what was happening but could not stop it. I don't even know if I would have stopped it, in all honestly. Father

249

Short Horror Stories Volume 3

Davies' head was peering through, staring towards the bed. Before he knew what was happening, I had his head in my hands and had snapped his neck where he stood.

I caught a glimpse of Father Benjamin rushing from behind the fallen priest, feebly attempting to close the door to my cell. With my new-found strength I beat him to it, kicking the heavy barrier wide open. I watched Father Benjamin stagger backwards before falling on his arse. He began muttering something in Latin, something that I couldn't understand but that the demon seemed to find hilarious. I could feel the deep rumbling laughter bounce about inside my mind before I realised it was coming out of my mouth as well.

I reached down, aiming for the crucifix around Father Benjamin's neck. As I snatched at it, I let out a scream, a terrifying combination of my own voice and the demon's. The holy symbol had burned my flesh. Father Benjamin took the opportunity to scramble to his feet and began to run, but I was faster. He had almost made it to the lift which I had used on the day I'd arrived, but I caught up with him, shoving him hard from behind. He fell forwards, banging his head against the metal door of the lift and seemed unconscious.

Ordinarily, this would have been enough for me, but my body was no longer my own. I watched in both horror and fascination as my right foot slammed into the back of Father

P.J. Blakey-Novis

Benjamin's skull, over and over, until I felt the crack of bone beneath my toes.

A matter of minutes later, I found myself exiting the lift and darting along the corridor towards freedom. I allowed myself a smile, felt a dull thud on the back of my head, and then all went black.

I came to on a bed not unlike the one my mother had just died in, my wrists and ankles bound by ropes tied to the frame beneath the thin mattress. I could feel the demon growling inside my head, thrashing about. I slowly opened my eyes, but I already knew what to expect.

Standing over me were three priests and a nun. They looked terrified and I recalled what Father Benjamin had told me when I demanded an exorcism for Sister Mary. *It's too expensive, we'd have to fly someone in from Rome.* This thought must have resonated with the demon, the knowledge that none of these holy men actually knew what they were doing.

As with the events since waking that morning, I could see, hear, and feel everything but had no control over it. I felt the demon's strength within me as though a physical entity were shoving my organs about. The ropes rubbed against my skin and my ears throbbed at the sound of the priests' muttering.

I fixed one of them with a stare, unable to look away as he, and his two companions,

251

Short Horror Stories Volume 3

recited a prayer in Latin over and again. I watched the nun, a pretty girl no older than twenty, step forward with a vial of water. As I spotted the crucifix on the vial the demon must have done the same as he recoiled within me. I let out an involuntary, deep scream as the cork was popped and burning drips of holy water were splashed across my face. The words of the priests seemed to have little effect, but that water was most unwelcome.

As if showing off his strength, I felt the demon elevate me from the rough mattress. I looked down the length of my body, seeing my feet bound at the ankles. My wrists remained fixed at the head of the bed but still I rose. I went to let out a scream, but no sound came. I continued to rise, at least the centre of me did, until my back had bent into an arch.

If my spine snaps then I'm dead, I yelled in my head. Immediately, I dropped. It seemed as though the priests only knew that one prayer and thought that if they repeated it consistently enough the entity would leave. Unfortunately, things weren't that simple. I don't know how long I lay there, writhing against my binds, but it felt like hours. I hadn't noticed the nun leave the room, but I did see her return, a leather-bound book in her hands.

"You boys need a fucking instruction manual?" I screamed in a voice not my own. I saw and felt myself spitting at them, but they paid me little attention. Huddled near the door, the four holy soldiers of God scanned the pages of *On the Sacred Rites of Exorcism*. There were mutters passed between them, punctuated by the occasional nod.

"Tell me your name," the lead priest demanded, finally facing the bed.

"Fuck off," I screamed.

"Tell me your name," he repeated. I let out the loudest roar imaginable and watched with satisfaction as the nun threw herself back against the wall. The priest, it seemed, was unfazed. He marched closer, his crucifix held out in front of him at arm's length. "Tell me your name, Son of Satan, in the name of Almighty God!"

"Rastrith," I heard myself say and I felt the entity weaken. Surprise registered on the face of the other priests and it fuelled their enthusiasm for the fight.

"In the name of the Lord God Almighty, and of Jesus Christ, and of the Holy Spirit, I command you, Rastrith, child of Satan, to leave this place."

I felt my body spasm, my fingers and toes curling in on themselves, my wrists and ankles pulling viciously at the ropes. The chanting began – what I thought was just from a movie was apparently the correct phrase.

"The power of Christ compels you!" Those words, shouted by four voices with as much conviction as they could muster, *did* have an effect of Rastrith. I could tell he wasn't

Short Horror Stories Volume 3

happy, and I only became more afraid. My innards were still being shoved about, my limbs contorting into unnatural shapes. There was a new pounding in my head, and I did not know if it meant anything – the discomfort was too much to bear.

"Mother fucking cunting bastard whore...." I heard escape from my mouth and I almost felt embarrassed at my profanity. I was no angel, but this seemed excessive. Still the priests continued and still the pain in my head grew. I felt as though my eyes were about to burst from their sockets. I felt my ears pop, as though there had been a change in air pressure. And then blackness came once again.

I awoke in the same position, still bound, and now incredibly sore. My back may not have broken, but I'd certainly torn a few important muscles. My wrists and ankles were raw with rope burns, my insides aches, but my headache had gone. Rastrith had gone.

"Hello," I called out, having found myself alone in the room. I was startled by my own voice, weak-sounding but human. I continued to call out until the nun, Sister Jennifer I soon learned, made an appearance. She looked at me with something resembling pity but it was tainted with something else...guilt, perhaps? Sister Jennifer had brought with her a glass of water and some biscuits which she placed on the small table

P.J. Blakey-Novis

beside the cot bed.

"Can you untie me please?" I asked, unsure as to why I was still being restrained. Silently, she pressed the glass of water to my mouth, allowing me to drink a little. She followed the water with one of the biscuits and made a hasty escape while I was busy chewing.

The noticeable difference between this room and my previous accommodation was the presence of a window. This allowed me to gain a better understanding of the time. When I had my first biscuit it had been dark. That had been three days ago, by my reckoning. I felt no presence within me as I lay on that now-filthy bed, marinating in my own piss. I'd hardly eaten so had managed to hold my bowels closed – a small mercy. The only visits were from the silent Sister Jennifer and I began to wonder if I'd ever leave. I had never expected to find myself in a worse situation than I'd been in previously, but here I was.

I think it had been a week, give or take a day or so either side, when *he* arrived. Elderly would be putting it kindly – the guy looked as though he were on the wrong side of one hundred. Dressed all in black, including a black Trilby hat, he was guided to my room by the priest who had driven out Rastrith. They spoke in hushed voices, casting worried looks in my direction.

"Who are you?" I asked, barely strong enough to open my eyes.

Short Horror Stories Volume 3

"It's unimportant, my dear," he said. "What *is* important, is what we do with you." His accent was hard to place so I figured he probably travelled a lot, but there was a hint of Italian in there and I'd put my money on him having arrived from Rome.

"Go home," is all I could manage, obviously referring to my desire to leave.

"We have a dilemma," the ancient one explained, his voice patronising. "You see, a lot has taken place here over the past ten days. I'm sure you can understand that the church would like it kept quiet."

"Because you've kept me locked up?" I said, trying to force some aggression into my voice.

"Partly," he conceded, "and we have lost some of our own in the battle. The church would like some, erm, assurances, that the events here won't become public knowledge."

I managed a nod and a short, "Of course." The man seemed undecided but even the church was not deceptive enough to hold me hostage like this indefinitely. It seemed they just needed someone higher up to make the decision to release me. I watched as the man's hands, shaking with age, pulled at the ropes which bound me. It felt as though it was taking hours and I expected him to call for help but he did not.

Eventually, my arms and legs were free, and I attempted to stand. The pain was almost unbearable but my desire to leave was greater.

P.J. Blakey-Novis

"I will show you to the shower room," the man explained, taking my arm. As we entered the corridor, he called for Sister Jennifer to assist me. I took the shower sitting down, under the watchful eyes of the nun. The warm water rushed over me and I sat there, eyes closed, trying to come up with an explanation to give my friends. Surely, I would be presumed dead by now?

Clean and in fresh clothes, Jennifer led me towards the exit of the *Mayfield Psychiatric Hospital*. The old man, the exorcist from the Vatican I suspected, was waiting at the door. He sent Sister Jennifer away and took my arm, leading me into the courtyard. It was the first time I had felt the sun on my skin in many weeks and it felt incredible. The priests may have been reluctant to let me go, but I had no intentions of discussing the events to anyone, ever.

Mr Exorcist, for I still didn't know his real name, walked beside me towards a waiting cab. We approached the gate and it opened automatically. I felt a pressure building in my head, that same start-of-a-headache feeling I'd felt during the exorcism.

"The cab will take you wherever you need to go," the man told me, gesturing towards the waiting vehicle. I looked at my ride, the driver of which was engrossed in a tabloid newspaper.

"Oh, I'll be going wherever I want," I said, in a low, guttural voice. "I'm just beginning." I saw my own arms reach out and snap the

Short Horror Stories Volume 3

brittle neck of Rome's best exorcist. Climbing into the cab, I gave the driver my address (in my own voice). He grunted in response, thankfully not noticing the corpse I'd left at the hospital's gate.

P.J. Blakey-Novis

Purgatory

1783, Cuckmere Haven, Sussex

I awoke to shouts coming from outside the small stone structure which I shared with my mother, father, and two younger sisters. Darkness was covering everything at this time of night, even the moon unable to pierce the layers of thick cloud. I sat myself up, careful not to disturb Elizabeth or Mary who slept through the hullabaloo, snuggled together for warmth on the rough blankets. I listened for movement inside the house, wondering if my father had heard the shouts. No sounds came from my parents' sleeping area, the sheet used as a partition remaining still.

As silently as I could manage, I turned myself over and pushed my face up to the cold stone of the wall, my right eye lined up with a small crack just large enough to see through. Father had promised Mother he would fill the gap a number of times but hadn't gotten around to it, the cold draught apparently not bothering him. It caused aches in my bones after sleeping beside the cold air, but I also valued the chance to gaze outside, so I never pressed the issue. Now, I was thankful for the small hole.

The loud, male voices seemed to be growing quieter and I couldn't tell if they were

Short Horror Stories Volume 3

becoming more distant or simply lowering their tones. I knew who they were, or rather, I knew *what* they were – smugglers. More specifically, *The Blues,* a gang I'd heard my father mention only in hushed tones and only to his brother, my Uncle Michael. It was unusual for these men, these *ungodly criminals* as Mother would call them, to be passing our home so brazenly.

Through the limited space between rocks, I could make out shadows trudging along the path, heading towards the steep entryway to Cuckmere Haven. The topography curved steeply, the path leading past our solitary home and descending sharply down to the valley floor. The river Cuckmere, a jagged finger of water, split the greenery in two and provided an easy entry point for *The Blues.*

The shouts which had awoken me must not have been signs of any altercation as the men continued on their way, dragging what looked like a farm gate behind them. It was too dark, and I was too slow in my rising, to discern how many smugglers there were but I'd counted at least twenty trudge past. *Should I wake Father?* I pondered, before dismissing the idea. He could be irritable at the best of times – with insufficient rest he would be worse. I settled myself back down to sleep, thoughts of smugglers and adventure filling my mind.

At breakfast, I couldn't keep silent about what I had seen. Cautiously, I waited until Father had swallowed the hunk of bread he

260

P.J. Blakey-Novis

was chewing, and then I began to tell him what I had seen. I told him everything, from the shouts to the shadowy processions heading towards the river, and my assumption that the men had been members of *The Blues*. I heard Mother tutting from her place beside the pot where she was busy preparing food for our later meal. Father was hard to read as he looked at me, a little puzzled perhaps, and waved off my news with his hand.

"I didn't hear a thing," he said. "And *The Blues* have no reason to be coming past here, so don't you worry about it."

"But," I pressed, ever cautious not to seem disrespectful, "don't they bring things in through the Cuckmere?" I already knew this was the case as Father had mentioned it to Uncle Michael not long ago. Father sighed.

"They do," he nodded, "but I don't believe it's a regular thing. And, whenever they have had business at the Cuckmere, they've always taken the route to the east, on the other side of the valley."

"So, it could have been them?" I said, as gently as I could.

"It is possible," Father agreed, reluctantly, "but very unlikely. I'd say it was your eight-year-old imagination, or just a dream. Don't get any fanciful ideas about the likes of *The Blues* – they are ruthless, greedy, dangerous men. They are not the sort of people a young man should look up to." I knew then that the conversation was over and wisely finished my

Short Horror Stories Volume 3

breakfast in silence.

The three weeks that followed were uneventful until we had a visit from Uncle Michael. His arrival wasn't anything out of the ordinary – he would come by to speak with father, usually with flowers for mother, each month or so. What was unusual was the late hour. As before, when I had been awoken in the night, the thick clouds prevented whatever moonlight existed from reaching the ground. I only knew of Uncle Michael's presence when I heard shouts, this time from inside the house. There was no mistaking his voice, nor that of Father, who sounded angrier than I had ever heard him.

The idea of leaving my bed never entered my mind, not wanting to get caught up in whatever disagreement the men were having. I could make out the silhouette of my mother, standing beside the sheet which led to her sleeping area. She could not tell that I was awake, and I suspected that she was eavesdropping on the disagreement too.

"You've lost your mind, brother," I heard my father yell. "After everything they have done, you want to join them? To help them, even!" I struggled to make out the response from Uncle Michael, his voice filled with a calmness which was in complete contradiction to my father's tone. "Then that's your decision," I heard Father continue. "But if this is the path you are choosing then you do not come by here

262

P.J. Blakey-Novis

again." A pause in the shouting followed, only the mumbled reply of my uncle could be heard. I thought I could make out the words '*Blues*' and '*opportunity*' but the context was lost on me.

Uncle Michael continued talking for what felt like hours, with Father remaining silent. Was he being talked into something? What had Uncle done to anger my father? I heard no more shouts before the door to our home slammed shut, the sound of hooves on soft earth passing by the crack in my wall.

I remained in my bed, watching my mother's shadow in the gloom as it moved to the door, opening it with a gentle creak. I could just about make out Mother's head turn towards me, checking to see if she had disturbed us, and I squeezed my eyes shut as though asleep. Satisfied that my siblings and I had not awoken, she slipped out the room. As soon as I heard the door pull closed, I strained my ears but could not make out any of the whispered words coming from beyond it.

There was a tension over breakfast with both Mother and Father seeming to be at odds with one another. They bickered very rarely; Father was headstrong, and Mother was happy to settle for a quiet life. Something had been discussed on that previous night, however, and Mother had put her foot down. The rarity of that act in itself meant that strange things were afoot and, as inquisitive

263

Short Horror Stories Volume 3

as I was, I knew I'd need to know more.

I held my tongue through breakfast, waiting for my father to head into town and run his errands. I've never known what this involved but he'd be gone for most of the day, three or four times a week. On the days he was with us, he'd be occupied working in the barn and taking care of general maintenance around the property. I was thankful today he would be gone and I could only pray my mother would be forthcoming with me.

"Are you alright?" I began, Mother looking surprised at my question. Perhaps I didn't ask about her wellbeing often, if ever.

"Of course I am, Thomas. Why wouldn't I be?"

"Have you and Father had an argument? You seemed angry with him over breakfast," I pressed. Mother smiled weakly, shaking her head.

"It's nothing for you to worry about," she said, helping Elizabeth with her clothing.

"But I am worried," I replied. "It has something to do with Uncle Michael, doesn't it?" This caught Mother off-guard, as I'd hoped.

"Why do you say that?" she asked, not denying my suggestion.

"I heard him arguing with Father last night, well, Father was arguing, I could barely hear Uncle Michael." Mother shook her head again, tutting this time.

"You know you shouldn't be eavesdropping on people, Thomas. It isn't proper."

264

P.J. Blakey-Novis

"You were," I blurted. "I mean, I could see you waiting to leave the room." Mother sighed, caught out by me.

"It's adult business and nothing to concern yourself with." Mother gave me a look which I knew meant I should drop it. Frustrated, I headed outside to play.

Weeks passed without any sign of *The Blues,* or Uncle Michael. I wondered, somewhat sadly, if Father had meant what he had said to Uncle about not being welcome at our home again. I had asked Father a few days previous, in my most innocent of tones, whether we would be seeing Uncle Michael again soon. Father grunted and changed the subject. Whatever the reason for that late-night visit and the subsequent disagreement, it appeared to have fractured the relationship between two close brothers. My eight-year-old mind could not fathom anything so serious. Until that night. The night when everything, and nothing, became clear. The night I learned answers but only gained more questions. The night Uncle Michael almost battered our door down.

The hammering of his fists on the wood was enough to rouse us all, even Elizabeth and Mary. Father almost leapt from his bed, dashing out of the room and closing the door behind him. Mother came to us, huddling us closely as though she knew danger were near. I heard Uncle Michael's distinctive voice in the entrance to our home, his pleas for

Short Horror Stories Volume 3

Father's help sounding desperate. I was in no doubt that something terrible had happened or was about to.

More shouting came from outside the house and I turned myself back towards the wall, one pupil, dilated with fear, scanning the area visible beyond. The moon was full and those clouds which had hung so heavy over previous weeks were nowhere to be seen. Everything out there could be seen for there was little darkness to hide *The Blues*.

The gang, perhaps forty or fifty strong, stormed to the front of our house. Mother's hands were clapped over the mouths of my sisters for fear of them crying out. I could every word clearly as Uncle Michael begged Father to join them.

"I need you," Uncle Michael said. "Don't resist, they will make you help us."

"You need to get out of my house," Father bellowed. "I told you last time – you're not welcome here. Not you, or this mob of criminals. I'll have nothing to do with your activities."

"We lost a shipment," Uncle Michael explained, his tone beginning to sound less panicked. "At the moment we don't know if it was seized but they never landed. Charles Radcliffe thinks you may have tipped off the authorities."

"You really are insane," Father replied, his voice taking on a nervous quiver. "You know I wouldn't do that. I'm well aware of what *The Blues* are capable of; why would I put my

266

P.J. Blakey-Novis

family in danger?"

"I told them that," Uncle insisted. "But once Charles gets an idea in his head it sticks. He said the only way he'll be able to trust you is if you come help us search for the shipment." There was a pause which must have been due to Father considering his options. Faced with a good forty ruthless killers, as he had often described them, it didn't sound as though he had any choice.

"And if I refuse?" Father asked. Someone else answered with a deeper, older sounding voice.

"If you refuse then you refuse. We'll leave you be," the stranger said. "After a few of my men have spent some quality time with your wife, of course!" The threat was followed by raucous laughter and I felt my mother recoil. Even though I did not understand the meaning of the threat, I sensed they meant to harm her. There was another moment of silence before I heard a crack, followed immediately by a gasp. "There will be a consequence for that, young man," I heard the voice say. He sounded pained and I wondered if Father had hit him.

"You need to come with us, for your family's sake," Uncle Michael said, and I heard Father's grunt of acceptance.

"And the boy," the older voice said, a voice I assumed belonged to Charles Radcliffe, infamous leader of *The Blues*.

"What?" Father asked. "You can't be serious! He's only eight, he'd be of no use to

267

Short Horror Stories Volume 3

you."

"Think of it as insurance," Charles replied. I could almost hear the smile on his face. "You do as we ask, we get our shipment, you and the boy come home. Anything seems off to me and he's the first one overboard." My heart thumped in my chest as I listened to the familiar stomp of my Father's feet approaching the bedroom.

"It'll be okay," he whispered to Mother. "Thomas, you stay right by my side the whole time. We'll be back before you know it."

My intrigue and, for want of a better word, admiration for *The Blues* disappeared as soon as we stepped into the night air. I managed a smile for Uncle Michael, but he only looked at the ground, his guilt spread thickly across his face. The man, Charles, apparent leader of this group of terrifying men, grinned at me with a toothless smile. The area beneath his nose was stained red, an injury I was certain Father had inflicted. I could only hope there would be no further repercussions for that act of violence.

I gripped Father's arm as we walked among the group, my fascination now having turned entirely to fear. The terror I felt as we were led towards the river was palpable, a part of me doubted we would even return to Mother and my sisters.

The path led alongside the riverbank and I felt the wet grass beneath my feet. The air was cool, but not uncomfortably cold and the moon and stars shone brightly. In other

P.J. Blakey-Novis

circumstances, it would have been a pleasant walk. I had no concept of what was required of us, or of Father in particular, so I remained silent and willed my hands to stop trembling.

We reached the mouth of the river, the grass turning to pebbled beach, and I saw the small boat that was waiting. Charles, who had remained close to us the whole way, chose this moment to speak.

"We'll be taking this vessel out to search for our missing cargo. Either the ship went down and our goods are floating about out there, or the authorities intervened. You'd best hope the ship sank," he said, looking my Father in the eye. "Otherwise, I'll have to wonder who got the authorities involved." His meaning was clear, even to me.

"When was the shipment due to arrive?" Father asked.

"Last night. The boys should have landed and brought the goods over to us, but they never showed. Fearing arrest, we stayed put until now."

"But even if the goods were lost at sea, they could be anywhere by now," Father said.

"Perhaps," Charles replied, not seeming all too bothered. "We should get a move on then. Either way, I'd like to know where my lads have got to."

The vessel was small, and I was relieved to see that not everyone was getting aboard. Charles led my Father and I onto the wooden boat, followed by Uncle Michael and three

Short Horror Stories Volume 3

men from his gang. I now understood the gist of what we needed to do; find the missing objects (the specifics of what they were was still unknown) and return them to shore. If we were unsuccessful then I knew something bad would happen, but I tried to focus on the job at hand. Thankful for the clear night, I began staring out to see, scanning the horizon for anything out of the ordinary.

Within twenty minutes I could no longer see the beach. The sea was calm, but its inky blackness still felt sinister, as though something awful waited beneath its surface. It must have been more than an hour before one of the men shouted that he could see something. The remaining six of us turned, facing the direction in which he was pointing. Relief swept over me as the large barrel bobbed gently along, only a few feet ahead. Uncle Michael and Father took the lead in retrieving the barrel and, after Uncle had almost fallen overboard, they were successful. As soon as the item was in the vessel, I felt the temperature drop. My back felt damp, or cold, or a combination of the two, so I turned. I could not see the other side of the boat, despite it being less than six feet away. The mist was too thick.

I felt its icy tendril surround me, seeming to muffle the sounds of the men onboard. I reached out my hands blindly, searching for Father, or even Uncle Michael. I tried to call out for Father, for anyone really, but the mist filled my mouth before I could make a sound.

P.J. Blakey-Novis

I felt its chill coating my tongue, numbing my throat and working its way down to my stomach. The boat jolted suddenly, as though it has beached, but that would be impossible. We were too far from the coast, but certainly not anywhere close to France. I'd never heard of any patches of land between the two coasts.

As quickly as it had arrived, the mist disappeared. Not in one instant, but it was as though it recoiled, pulled away by some unseen hand in the darkness. I found Father, only inches away from me, and I clung on to him. Everyone seemed confused, disorientated, but nobody knew what to say. Around the boat were more barrels, and the sight of them seemed to bring Charles back to his senses as he ordered his men to start dragging them aboard.

"We hit something," I whispered to Father. He nodded, looking around. There was nothing obvious – no rocks jutting out of the ocean and certainly no land.

"Perhaps it was the barrels we struck," he suggested, but he did not seem to believe his own words. "Stay put, I'm going to help. The sooner we get this done, the sooner we'll be home." I did as I was told, remaining fixed to the spot through fear as much as obedience. My eyes were the only things to move, darting around the surface of the water, checking how many barrels were left, keeping a watch for monsters.

The men made quick work of retrieving

271

Short Horror Stories Volume 3

their lost goods and I sensed a communal fear within the group. Whatever had brought that unnatural mist upon us had shaken everyone; even the bold and fearless leader of *The Blues* seemed to be hiding a nervousness as he barked orders. When all the loot was aboard, Charles gave the order to return to shore.

One of Charles' men, a huge brute of a man with a scar across his throat, piped up. "Something isn't right, boss. The compass, it's ... it's spinning." Even I knew he must have meant the needle, but it was still concerning. I watched Charles grab the thing and check it himself. The other men gathered around, Father included, so I took a step forward. Sure enough, the needle was spinning, full circles, over and again. I knew what that meant just as much as every man onboard – we were lost.

Charles stared into the night sky, reading the stars. From the little I knew of smugglers, they were rarely sailors. More often than not, they were just thugs who brought goods inland once they arrived on a beach. I could see a look of puzzlement of Charles' face but, of course, I dared not question his methods. He pointed, unconvincingly, in one direction and his men followed the order. I wondered if they thought he knew what he was doing, or if they just felt that any direction was as good a suggestion as any other.

The three *Blues* and Uncle Michael took to the oars, rowing further into the night. Mere

272

minutes passed before I felt that icy chill again and I knew what was happening. Quickly, I grabbed Father's arm, holding on as tightly as I could, afraid the mist would somehow tear us apart. I heard muffled voices once again. Then the screaming began.

The first scream came from my left, where the giant with the scarred neck had been rowing. It sounded like an angry roar, but it was as though it came from far way, not the few feet actually between us. Through the mist I could just about make out the silhouette of the man, flailing his arms about, before the unmistakable sound of a splash echoed through. He'd gone overboard but the fog was too dense for any of us to see him.

More muffled cries came through the curtain of damp white, more shadows of men dancing about the boat. All the while, Father held his position and I clung to him with all my might. More splashes followed, silencing the screams. I was unsure if I heard four or five, which meant I did not know if Uncle Michael was still onboard. I scrunched my eyes tightly, willing this horror to end. As though it had obeyed me, the mist retreated in the same way it had previously. Uncle Michael was nowhere to be seen and Father and I were faced with only Charles.

He looked afraid, and rightly so. The unearthly mist and its decimation of his crew aside, Charles now found himself facing my Father's wrath. There was nothing stopping my Father from taking his revenge on the

Short Horror Stories Volume 3

man who had threatened his wife and subjected his son to this nightmarish journey. I could feel my Father's arm tense, as though about to strike. He shook his head.

"If we survive this, Charles," Father said, "I want to hear nothing from you or your men again."

"Agreed," Charles muttered, and for once he sounded sincere. The three of us scrambled along the sides of the boat, searching for the fallen men. Charles called out for his men while Father and I searched for Uncle Michael. There was no sign of any of them, no shouts for helps, no ripples in the water, no floating corpses. It was as if the sea had taken them completely, swallowing them whole.

"Have you got the compass?" Father asked, his voice filled with authority. Charles pulled it from his pocket, holding it out to Father. The men watched it as the needle settled, then nodded at one another.

"Thomas, I'll need you to grab an oar," Father told me. I had no idea what I was doing but Father looked at me kindly. "Just do your best, any help is better than none."

We rowed in the direction of north until my hands were blistered. I held in the pain, not wanting to let Father down. Having seen these smugglers up close, having been exposed to them so clearly, I could now see who should receive my admiration. Father was a good man; intelligent, brave, and honest. I rowed as hard as my body would let

P.J. Blakey-Novis

me, shoulders throbbing, back aching, until I heard Charles shout.

"There!" he screamed, the joy flowing from his mouth. I looked ahead of us and could just make out the flames of torches on a beach. We'd made it back to Cuckmere Haven and I was thankful that Charles had made it too. It would have been hard to explain to his men how we'd returned without any of the crew.

The light of the flames grew brighter and I guessed we were maybe a hundred feet from shore, if that. My relief was short lived as those icy tendrils appeared as if from nowhere, feeling more like fingers than ever before. I looked towards Father and Charles, rowing with their backs to me, and I tried to scream. The sound caught in my throat as I felt the cold, white hand squeeze my windpipe. Things were different this time – the boat was not filled with mist, Father was unaware of my situation. The mist had come only for me and I could not move nor make a sound.

I could still see the flames of the torches ahead and we were getting closer. Father and Charles seemed to be deep in concentration, not paying any attention to my plight. I felt the mist surrounding me completely as it blocked my vision. I dropped the oar, but the splash didn't reach my Father's ears. I couldn't see, couldn't scream, and I was certain I would die.

Perhaps I did. For the mist enveloped me

Short Horror Stories Volume 3

so completely that I felt my body lift within it. I struggled for breath, the cold shards of vapour penetrating my lungs. I felt as though I were floating. The mist began to thin in front of my eyes and, if I had been able to, I would have let out a scream. I saw Father and Charles, rowing the boat, almost at the shore. Only I was no longer in it. I was there, within the fog, above the surface of the sea. I watched as Father and Charles moved further away and felt a tear escape from my eye, freezing on its way down my cheek.

I felt a rush of air as the mist disappeared towards the horizon, taking me with it. As the cold enveloped me, crushing me, I was overcome by darkness. Perhaps I died, but maybe I didn't. Everything is cold and dark, but my mind still remains active. Could this be purgatory?

Acknowledgements

Rosebud Cottage first published in *B is for Beasts,* Red Cape Publishing, 2020

Alone No More first published in *In Uterus,* Planet Bizzaro Press, 2022

Something Foul on Floor Thirteen first published in *Castle Heights*, Red Cape Publishing, 2021

The Pioneer first published in *A is for Aliens,* Red Cape Publishing, 2020

The Tom Booker Sessions first published in *F is for Fear,* Red Cape Publishing, 2020

Break-In at St. Benedict's first published in *Sweet Little Chittering,* Red Cape Publishing, 2021

Doomsday first published in *Old Scratch: Demon Tales & Devil Hells*, Crimson Pinnacle Press, 2022

The Long Con first published in *The Horror Collection: Sapphire Edition,* KJK Publishing, 2022

Short Horror Stories Volume 3

Rise of a Fucking Superstar first published in *Unceremonious*, Red Cape Publishing, 2022

Carver's Hill first published in *C is for Cannibals,* Red Cape Publishing, 2020

Blurred and Fractured Memories first published as a standalone short story on Godless Horrors independently, 2022

We Want to Sing You a Song first published in *Collected Christmas Horror Shorts III*, KJK Publishing, 2023

Sister Mary first published in *D is for Demons,* Red Cape Publishing, 2020

Cassie and the Demon first published in *E is for Exorcism*, Red Cape Publishing, 2020

Purgatory is exclusive to this collection and was originally written for a local anthology that sadly never went to print.

P.J. Blakey-Novis

Other Titles

Short Horror Stories Volume 1

Short Horror Stories Volume 2

Four: A Horror Novella

**Demons Never Die: Artwork & Flash
Fiction**

**Six Days of Violence: Artwork & Flash
Fiction**

Printed in Great Britain
by Amazon